PIECES

PIECES a collection of new voices

edited by STEPHEN CHBOSKY

POCKET
BOOKS
NEW YORK LONDON TORONTO SYDNEY

An *Original* Publication of MTV Books/Pocket Books

POCKET BOOKS, a division of Simon & Schuster Inc.
1230 Avenue of the Americas, New York, NY 10020

ISBN: 0-671-00195-7

First MTV Books/Pocket Books trade paperback printing August 2000

10   9   8   7   6   5   4   3

POCKET and colophon are registered trademarks of
Simon & Schuster Inc.

Art Direction and Design: Stacy Drummond
Photography: Jason Stang

Printed in the U.S.A.

CONTENTS

In the spring of 1998, I was working a temp job, and my boss hated me. I didn't particularly blame him for this, considering I stayed up all night writing and arrived every morning bleary eyed from lack of sleep between ten to fifteen minutes late as a result. When I finally did show up, if I wasn't using the Internet to check basketball scores or NFL draft picks, I was calling my friends and daydreaming of a time when I would not be crushed by poverty and debt. It was on a Thursday that my boss told me not to use the phone for personal calls anymore, even if I was using my calling card and even if he had nothing better for me to do. It was on a Friday that I "bent" this rule and received what would become my last personal phone call at that office. It was my friend Heather, and I only remember her saying one thing:

"They want to publish your book, Steve."

I had learned not to get my hopes up. I had learned that in the great lottery of artistic chance, if you hear that the head of Pocket Books is going to read your manuscript by the end of the week, give her about three weeks, and don't be surprised if she says no. As a matter of fact, count on it, and then pick yourself up the next day and keep trying. Keep temping. Keep writing.

I stayed on that phone call (to the delight of my boss) for an hour and a half just to make sure that it was real—that someone, somewhere wasn't playing some cruel joke. When I was finally convinced, I hung up the phone, all numb and smiles, and went to my boss's office.

"Sir, I'm sorry I was on a personal call, but here's the thing . . . That was Heather, who's dating my friend Chris, and she got it to Eduardo and Jack, who went to college with her, and they all created a grass roots campaign with Greer . . . and long story short . . . they're going to publish my book, *The Perks of Being a Wallflower.*"

After he smiled and said a genuine congratulations, I went outside to enjoy the last ten minutes of my lunch hour. I was flying on so much excitement that I don't remember the walk, the elevator, who I saw, anything. All I remember is that it was cold as hell and windy, and I found myself a little corner next to the building near a courtyard where nobody would be inclined to look. There I let everything settle. I let all that adrenaline calm down. And I cried my eyes out.

I had been writing for a long time. I had made a movie. I had worked for Hollywood studios. But this was different. This was my book and my main character, Charlie, who meant the world to me. This was a singular wish. And someone out there had said yes.

I finished my work that afternoon. I put a rib dinner on American Express that night. And everything was right in the world. Ten months later, after another dinner, I went with my sister Stacy into a bookstore, and for the first time, I saw my book on the shelves. That green cover and picture of the boy's legs, my name, and the title.

All I could say was, "There it is."

I didn't know what would happen to it. I didn't know if anybody would read it. All I knew was that it was out there, and as long as it was out there, there was a possibility.

So, when Greer Kessel Hendricks, who is my editor and dear friend, asked me to write an introduction to this collection, all I could think about were the fifteen young authors whose stories appear in this book walking into their local bookstores with their friends and families and saying:

"There it is."

Then, I thought about the possibility for them. And for you. And I congratulate all persons involved. Because whether you picked up this book because you love short stories, are interested in young authors, thought the cover looked good, or want to hate it, you have it. It's in your hands right now. And there is a possibility that somewhere in these pages, you may discover something special. Something honest. Well-crafted. Messy.

For a long time, I have thought about the great American authors and literary movements. I've wondered what made them different. What made them special. Was it hard work, drink, brash arrogance, ambition both personal and professional? Was it their belief in an honest sentence, their schooling, their culture? Was it time? Or was it simply that some publisher liked what he or she read and put it out there and let the readers decide for themselves?

I have looked for an answer to these questions as long as I've been writing because it is my hope that the writers of today and tomorrow will strive for such work along with the musicians, filmmakers, painters, sculptors, and all the other artists out there.

As difficult and breakneck as our society can be at times, it is my belief that we can have that community, and all it takes is someone creating something, someone else being willing to put it out there, and someone else being willing to look at it for what it is. That's where it all starts and where it all ends. It is you with this book in your hand, ready to turn the page to the first story and see what you think of it. And then turning the page to the next story and the next. With that one gesture, you will be a part of what may be a discovery. What may be a new movement. A new voice to celebrate. With that one gesture, you contribute to the belief that there is always hope in the young.

And if you hate it, well, what the hell. There's always tomorrow.

Stephen Chbosky
May 16, 2000

PIECES

So then I said,

"Would it make you *happier* if I were . . . wringing my hands? Mumbling about . . . the inescapable malaise of mankind's existential torpor . . . darting eyes, furrowed brow?! That sort of thing? Or maybe I should do my best Jack Nicholson? I mean, hey, we've *all* been to college. We've all read . . . *Dora.* Between the lines, right?"

To which this straight-faced white-coat, with her hair pulled so tightly against her scalp that I thought (wished) her eyes were going to pop out of their sockets, crossed her annoyingly svelte legs, reperched her goddamned Kata frames atop her unaccommodating third-world nose, and asked, "You said 'happier'; what makes you think that any of this makes me happy?"

"Listen," I demurred, "I'm really a docile person. In fact," I laughed (alone), "I'm probably more alarmed at my little outburst than you are. An outburst that—I think it's only fair to say—is an obvious manifestation of a severe anxiety attack, which, really, is all I've been trying to tell you."

"You said 'alarmed.' And why do you think that any of this would alarm me?"

Oh no. This shrink's laconic turnarounds were getting on my nerves. Two hours in the emergency waiting room for *this* shit? I should have kept right on walking, past Columbia Medical and straight up to

Harlem, where they keep the chitchat to a minimum, and the closest thing to a Rorschach test is deciphering the spray-painted tags on tenement walls. Too bad it was snowing. And too bad the brothers didn't take Blue Cross.

She waited for an answer, and I briefly closed my heavy eyes. Stay calm. Keep it together. You've prepared for this.

And I had: tales of depressions and promotions and scary dreams; veiled admissions (because you have to give them a *taste* of what they want to hear) of maybe drinking a tad too much. Throughout my rehearsed tour-de-force, of course, I affected a look of humility and puppy dog perplexity: I guess it's *society,* because—Lord knows—it's not *my* fault the boss takes me out to after-work-Vodka-Martini-shoot-the-shit sessions. Yes, I went all the way, trying my best for POSTER BOY: ABSOLUTE ANXIETY.

On my walk (sprint) to the ER, I actually imagined their thoughts upon meeting me: *I wonder what could be troubling this sweet sweaty little white boy that he's here all alone during a snowstorm. Things must be rough, I'd better load him up with some good drugs. Come 'ere baby.* Simple!

Simple, that is, until I ran into this shrink, who, at midnight no less, felt the irrepressible need to plague me with her mealy-mouthed rhetoric. What's to talk about?! She was skeptical as to my sincerity—I could smell that a mile away. And *sure,* I got a little out of hand last night but, come on. I mean, what would you have done in my situation?

It's three in the morning, and you're at this party on the Lower East Side, high above Stanton Street, in one of those artist's lofts that you read about in *New York* magazine (football fields' worth of hardwood floors; original Basquiats on the exposed brick walls; beautiful, exotic Barneys play soundlessly on jumbo monitors—in fact, Matthew himself is bumming cigarettes from you; a balcony view of the river and World Trade and Jersey, et al) with every model and eccentric erudite in Manhattan who just happen to be offering you everything from E to Cristal mimosas. *What do you do*? Right! You ingest, ingest, ingest. So come sunrise, when you can't fuck (or, even say, talk), and your pupils are on permanent strobe effect, a few bong hits don't seem like such a terribly bad idea.

But later, at the office, you're shaking like Los Angeles during the Big One, and decide to head home a little early. You're in bed by noon and it's just not working out. You're exhausted but doing somersaults in the sheets. Your brain is in the mood to exercise. You can't stop thinking. So as the soupy afternoon settles into a starless night, as the hours trudge away, you try a few things to calm down. Reading—all those words. Television—all those expensive teeth. Radio—all those DJs. Phone call—all those answering machines. E-mail—all those Forwards. Whip up some gourmet masterpiece in the kitchen—all those empty cupboards. Bike ride—all that snow. Laundry—all that dirt. Meditate—all that impossibility. Pray—all that nothingness. Masturbate—all that work. More drugs—*Hey.* Wait a minute.

Drugs? Drugs. That's not a bad idea. Why didn't you think of that before? What, though? Everyone you know will just have poisonous hallucinogenics or volcanic amphetamines. You need barbiturates. Two blue beauties and a tall glass of ice water. Good clean pharmaceuticals to slow things down. You're freaking out! Six blocks away is Columbia Medical.

You can do it. You look in the mirror, a quick run through the likely interrogative stumbling blocks—give it your best shot! Let's go! And so you go.

And so I went.

"Look, I'm sorry, Miss . . . ?"

"Singh. Dr. Singh."

"Of course. Dr. Singh, I feel awful that we seem to be miscommunicating here. I'm sure it's just . . . semantics and we can . . . parley this into something rewarding for us both. I mean, after all, we're both ultimately concerned with the same thing—mental health. In my opinion, too many people in today's society give mental health insufficient attention. It's a shame, really, when you think about the millions of innocent people who are suffering, don't you think? I mean, thank God there are dedicated, compassionate people, like yourself, helping to ease the terrible burden of mental anguish."

"You were maybe . . . partying it up last night?"

Fuck!

"Partying it up?! No! . . . Well, okay, I guess I did have one too many glasses of wine; my limit's two. It . . . well, it was a dinner party for two of my friends who just got back from their honeymoon in—" I quickly searched the room for clues, of which there was an alarming dearth (bookless, degreeless, wedding-ringless, pictureless, plantless—*lifeless*—oh, those clever, clever doctors). "—Their honeymoon in *New Delhi,* which they loved, by the way, and anyway, we were all so happy for them that I guess I got a little carried away."

There was a thundering silence.

"I guess, Dr. Singh, that if I really stop and think about it, that's why I'm here tonight." I was looking at the floor, and, to my surprise (and anger—I needed to believe I was only acting), my voice actually began to waver. Does this make sense, getting choked up over my own bullshit? No, it does not. I concluded with an Oscar-worthy performance that would have made Brando jealous. "Seeing two people so happy . . . I'm twenty-five, this is my second year out of college . . . I'm not getting any younger. And it's just made me reconsider love and wonder if I'll ever find it out there."

I peered up and for the first time saw the scope of her forever-brown eyes magnified by her elegant frames—they said safety, they said commiseration. They said drugs.

"Young man, this is what I am thinking . . ." and, when she paused and actually leaned over the table to touch her palm to my wet wrist, I inwardly grew exalted. I was singing a song of Victory, envisioning my spongy, dreamless sleep, when she concluded, "I am thinking that you've beleaguered yourself with illegal narcotics, and it has caught up with you. I think you are here tonight in a vulgarly transparent attempt to score some pharmaceutical antianxiety medication. It's late and there was probably nowhere else to go. I'm not the person to help you."

When she said "score" I wanted to rip her throat out. *Score*. My *God*, she probably read that word in the *Stanford Review of the Self-Medicating Junkie's Vernacular* or something.

"But," devastated and enraged, I asked (actually wanting to know), "what am I going to do?"

"Well, you are going to seek therapy, I hope. And quite obviously you should stop self-medicating."

And *there-it-is*, I thought. The perennial paradox of all those sententious bloodsuckers practicing mental health: Seek therapy, where you will be told by your shrink that it is not their responsibility to provide you with the answers, they are merely a guide for your journey to self-awareness, self-discovery. The answers lie in you and you alone. Yet *they're* the ones who decide when and if you need a fucking Band-Aid!

Well, let me say this: It doesn't take a neuroscientist or Carl Fucking Jung to tell me that I've *discovered* that I feel like shit tonight. Yes. Yes, I beleaguered myself last night with drugs and booze. And to that I ask in all sincerity, *So what?* That fact doesn't assuage the fact that *tonight* my physical discomfort has escalated to the point of cerebral gridlock—I'm stuck in my mind, but the motor's turning and I'm running out of fucking gas. This is emotional. This is real. I'm obsessing over everything from reincarnation to what kind of bagel I should buy on my way to work tomorrow. My heart's on overdrive. No brown paper bag or walk through the park is going to fix this. I'm dreary . . . I'm elated! I hate what I've done . . . I can't live without it! I'm losing it . . . I'm a winner! I'm a crybaby . . . I'm a hero! I'm lost . . . I'm right here! I'm inside . . . out! And what all this very simply means is—I need a fucking Xanax and I need it right fucking now!

I was at the end of my rope.

But—get this—then I started to cry. But—get *this*—I wasn't faking it—Oh no. I cried for real. In fact, not true. I wept. I sobbed an Amazon of salty currents and snotty slipstreams. I bawled all over the place. I gushed and snuffled because I knew I was done for; she saw through me as easily and acutely as a tenth-grader sees through his date's sheer blouse. And like the date, who feels stupid for putting herself there in the first place, who feels enervated for her backfiring attempt at seduction, I felt cheap. No damn good.

I choked up my pathetic tears and, though I knew it futile, thought, why the hell *not*. I went for some of the tenth-grade stuff myself.

With the last tears in my eyes I looked up and stared out of Dr. Singh's ugly hospital window, and softly said, "To tell you the truth, my mother died a month ago, today. She had cancer. Bone cancer, actually. The ironic thing is, that's not even what got her. While she was driving to her chemo appointment, a . . . a tractor-trailer broadsided her Honda. We . . . we identified her by her dental records. Sometimes I think that that was probably better, but . . . I don't know, I guess I'm just not dealing very well." Then I paused and turned to Dr. Singh. "And you were right, there *was* no place else to go. And it's late."

Zip. Nada. Zero.

I forgot about the scoring game (for now I was awesomely afraid of facing those unfriendly sheets; my every nerve ending a burning matchstick, illuminating my anxieties, searing my skin; the falling snowflakes crushing my eardrums; the purgatory of trying to just hit the hay). I stood up, and Dr. Singh removed her expensive glasses.

With that simple gesture her eyes shrank to human size.

"Are you familiar with the author Saul Bellow?"

Oh *no.*

"Uhm, yeah. But listen—"

"There is a line of his that I find quite interesting. Would you like to hear it?"

Sure. Oh, yeah. That's exactly what I'd like. I stood there and forced a smile.

"'People are like the faces on a playing card, upside down either way you look at them.' Do you know what that means? I think it means that it's an arduous, perhaps futile endeavor to try and get a person's straight face. To get the truth. Well, I've taken that endeavor and I think it's an important one. I look at you, and I certainly don't doubt that you are suffering."

My eyes darted to life. This is it!

"But unfortunately, I do doubt that you are telling the truth."

Or not.

"I'm not an easily deceived person, you see. However, as with playing cards, it is part of my job to risk, to gamble. I'm going to take a chance with you in light of what you have just told me, and hope that you, not I, turn out to be the winner."

She sighed a somewhat obnoxious, effusive sigh, the meaning of which I cared not to decipher, and magically produced the Little White Notepad on which she jotted down a string of intimidating-looking letters and numbers like X's and 7's, and gracefully signed her name.

Well whaddaya know.

She told me it was still against her better judgment, but considering my recent hardship she was going to write me a prescription for five Atavan—an antianxiety that would help me get some rest, which I desperately needed, she hastened to add.

She tore the page from the pad. I tensed.

"One last thing," she said. "If I gamble on you, and lose—I lose a lot more than professional integrity. I lose someone who came to me, presumably, for help. I lose a person. I lose you. It will be my mistake. My misjudgment. Put simply, using our gambling analogy, if you're lying to me about your mother just to get drugs, I will have misread your face, and lost big. But I will also get back in the game—the game of helping people. And if you do 'win' with some ace up your sleeve—so be it. But remember, if that's the way you're playing, the stakes are going to be a hell of a lot higher than what's sitting on the table."

She looked at me as though waiting for something.

"I'm telling you that if there is anything you truly want to say, anything that you don't understand, anything frightening you, now would be an ideal time. The time is now. I think you understand."

"I'd just like to say . . . well, it's just . . ."

"Yes?" she asked in a voice softer than sleep.

I suddenly felt the room spin; a confessional magnet was sucking at my burdens and lies; she looked like an angel. What was I doing?

"It's just . . . it's just great that we finally understand each other. Thanks. Thanks a million."

Whew. This close.

She handed me the slip of paper and, looking vaguely disappointed, started in on her paperwork.

The nearest all-night pharmacy was on 93rd Street and Broadway, fifteen blocks and three avenues away in a snowstorm at one in the morning with work in less than seven hours. I started walking.

When I got to the pharmacy, I was shaking and my feet were wet and my heart was pounding and my blood was hungry for chemicals.

When the pharmacist heard the rinkydink, up-for-the-holidays doorbell announce my entrance, he put down his paperback book and said more to the front door than to me, "Someone's pourin' it on pretty thick out there tonight, huh?"

"You betcha."

As I handed the pharmacist my prescription, which I had, of course, doctored from five to twenty-five, I thought about Dr. Singh: the literary Indian woman with nice legs and an M.D. in Clinical Psychiatry who was quicker to prescribe drugs for an appalling textbook lie than she was for good-intentioned half-truths. What a sucker. She hoped I was the winner? Not too tough when someone throws the game.

After I gave the man my money, he handed me the sepia container of pills. I made my way to the exit and laughed as I thought of Dr. Singh again. Yes, what a shame, what a nearsighted sucker, I thought, as I pushed open the door and squinted in the glare of streetlights bouncing off an unplowed, flakes-six-inches-deep Broadway. It had stopped snowing and somehow kids making angels and cabs cartwheeling slush hadn't yet gotten to the snowfall. The snow was immaculate. A virginal blanket tucking in the big bad city.

I admired it, then walked approximately half of a block before I realized how long and bone-cold and jittery the rest of the walk home would be.

I quickly popped two pills and tried to dry-swallow them. I was so dehydrated that it felt like trying to swallow a couple of mothballs covered in peanut butter. They wouldn't budge.

So it was exactly here—on the southeast corner of 94th Street and Broadway, at an indeterminately late hour, with drugs stuffed under my tongue—that I knelt down, stuck my hands into that perfect blanket of snow, and shoveled past my chapped lips fistful after fistful of that cooling, brilliant wetness.

That is to say, it was here that I finally swallowed the cocktail I had fought so hard to get.

And then I waited. I waited for the ebb of sensation, the fuzzy whispers of a drugged mind, the illusion of peace.

And then I felt the snow melting onto my legs; I felt the wind ripping past my ears; I felt the emptiness in and around me; I felt every miserable inch of the real world from which I was trying to escape, and then it dawned on me like a blast of hungover sunshine: I had gulped down sugar pills. I dumped the remaining pills into my hand and stared in horror at what I saw: big white dum-dums. The austere equation on Dr. Singh's magic pad had added up to PLACEBO.

I laughed. Slumped in the snow, soaked and alone for blocks, I laughed. I laughed for so long and so hard at the good doctor's funny funny joke (to wit, *she knew I was lying the whole time, and the only medicine she wrote a prescription for was a taste of my own*—ha ha ha ho ho ho hee hee hee!!!) that eventually, as I completely fell apart and was swept away by fatigue, eventually the idea of falling asleep sober—the idea of falling into a dreamy nonchemical bliss where I am safe—eventually the idea seemed plausible.

It is May Day in Paris. The sky is gray, almost purple. It is raining. Drizzling. The usual numbers of people flock to the Eiffel Tower. The tower looks the same as it always has except for one thing. On the top of the iron structure, a large red heart has seemingly been impaled there. Really it is made of fiberglass and supported by beams running through its middle that attach it to the tower. The spire and top observation deck poke out of the top of the heart. An artist has put this heart here. He had a vision seven years ago, and after years of construction and convincing the French government to allow him to put the heart on the tower, his vision has been realized. A huge heart has been stabbed by the Eiffel Tower.

People line up underneath the tower to buy tickets to go to the top. They want to see the City of Lights from the observation deck. It sounds funny, but people have funny thoughts. The light rain hasn't stopped these people from coming to the tower. In their minds and sometimes out loud they say, It will pass.

The grass in the esplanade in front of the tower is green and the trees there are becoming green. Spring is arriving slowly this year in Paris. It is still cold. Not cold enough for snow, but cold. There is a slight breeze. If it weren't raining it might be considered a comfortable day.

Some people are carrying lilies. May Day is Labor Day in Paris, and lilies are a Labor Day tradition. The tourists wonder what the lilies mean. Some find out that they are a symbol of spring. Others are too afraid to ask.

The people who are not waiting to ascend the great tower are at least looking up at it. They are taking pictures of it or marveling at the immense heart that takes up close to two thirds of the top section of the tower, the section above the second observation deck. Tickets can be bought for access to any observation deck. The higher the deck, the higher the price. There are three observation decks on the tower. One elevator stops at the first and second, and another carries passengers from the second to the third. It is also possible to climb to the first and second decks by way of stairwells located in two legs of the tower. The top deck is strictly elevator business. Because of the magnitude of the structure, it is advised that those afraid of heights remain firmly rooted to the ground.

At the ticket window an elderly Swedish couple buys tickets to go to the top. She decides to ride to the top; he decides to climb to the second deck, where, he says, he'll meet her so they can ride to the top together. She asks him if he's going to be okay climbing the stairs. He gives her a funny look and tells her he isn't as old as he looks. She smiles at him. He takes the Olympus camera from around his neck and gives it to his wife. Be careful, she tells him. He says, Wait for me. He walks to one of the legs closest to the esplanade, the one with the only open stairwell on this day. He begins to climb. It is 16h09. The stairs in the Eiffel Tower do not close until 18h00.

A young woman in a brown sweater and black skirt watches the man make his way up the first flights. His sweatshirt is very ugly, she thinks. She is leaning on a signpost. She looks back at the people under and around the tower. They're always in groups, she thinks. They're always with other people who look alike. She focuses on a small boy who is holding his mother's hand. I want a child, the woman thinks. No, I don't.

The boy's mother points to the air. She asks the seven-year-old if he likes the big heart on the tower. He answers, No, it scares me. I like it, the mother tells her child. Okay, he says. The boy looks at a man selling candy from a cart and says, Can I have a sweet?

The man with the candy cart has sold candy underneath the Eiffel Tower for almost seven years. The man with the candy cart is unshaven and hates kids. He hates his job. He thinks it's dirty and uncivilized. It always rains here, he thinks, but they still come. I wish the rain would melt them, he thinks. I wish they'd all flow away, down the Seine to the ocean, or to wherever the Seine goes. Two suckers, a woman says to him. *Bien sûr,* the man answers.

Some people think standing underneath the tower will prevent them from getting wet. It helps, but the wind is really the deciding factor. The breeze blows to the north today, so the further north people stand, the dryer they remain. But the tower is made of open iron work, so water still penetrates. People sometimes forget that. A man with piercing green eyes and a tattoo of a snake wrapped around a sword on his upper right arm makes his way to the center of the area underneath the tower. When he gets to what he believes is the exact center, he kneels, takes his black backpack off, and opens it. He pulls out an original Polaroid SX-70 Land Camera in mint condition. He looks through the viewfinder and points the camera directly up. He presses the red button and gets an instant picture of the underside of the tower.

The man with the candy cart sees him and laughs. He looks across the space beneath the tower to the leg opposite the one he is nearest. The man selling *chiens chauds* has a line at his cart. Fucking America, the candy man thinks.

The man selling these *chiens chauds* or, literally, hot dogs, squeezes mustard onto one of his wares. He looks at the hot dog and thinks, If this is pig, then I'm the Pope. He hands the hot dog to the English tourist who ordered it. With a forced smile and a heavy French accent, he says, Enjoy.

There are three women named Joy at the Eiffel Tower today. All are from America, but none knows any of the others. One is disappointed at the top of the tower. The clouds are ruining a potentially breathtaking view. One is reading a Metro map. She is on line with her son to buy tickets. She is studying the map intently hoping she will not get lost and miss her meeting with her husband at their hotel at 6:30. Her husband said he was going to spend the day at the Louvre or some museum, but he is on La Rue Saint Denis looking at other things. The third Joy is on the first elevator, which is making its way up one of the iron legs from the first observation deck to the second.

The third Joy stands next to a woman who has a camera around her neck. Joy thinks the woman looks Dutch. These two women are looking out the window of the large elevator. The elderly Swedish tourist, who is the woman standing next to Joy, is excited to be making this ascension. She wonders how long it will take her husband to climb all those stairs to meet her. From the elevator, she cannot see the leg of the tower in which her husband has just begun to have a heart attack. She is instead focused on someone down below holding a bright red umbrella. It sticks out amongst the mostly black umbrellas in the crowd. How nice, she thinks.

The woman who is holding the red umbrella is dressed in a red wool sweater and a black silk skirt. Her full lips are red, and her long, wavy hair is black. She is a twenty-six-year-old struggling playwright. She has come to the Eiffel Tower today to see the heart one of her favorite artists has put on top of the tower. Now she is waiting for her friend who lives in Montparnasse and whom she is staying with in Paris to come meet her. They set to meet at 4:30. It is 4:14. Screams from one of the far legs of the tower register in her head. She does not turn to look. Instead, she thinks, Art has gotten big.

As she searches her purse for a cigarette, a twenty-four-year-old man approaches her. *Est-ce que vous parlez anglais?* he asks.

I'm American, she answers. With the hand that isn't holding the umbrella, she puts a cigarette in her mouth and lights it with a red lighter. Why are you talking to me? she thinks. She usually doesn't mind talking to strangers, but she is not in an outgoing mood today.

Really? the man asks. From where?

New York, she answers. She blows smoke to the left of his head. She is taller than he is. He is wearing a black pullover with black jeans and a dark green jacket. He's not bad-looking, she thinks, but those ears.

He nods. She is stunning, he thinks. Even a gay man could be persuaded. Me too, he tells her. It's nice to hear English, he continues. The French don't like to speak English.

Yeah, she says. That's because they're French, she thinks.

And they don't like it when I try to speak French, he says.

I think they appreciate when you try, she tells him. She wants to say, What do you need so I can tell you and you can leave me alone?

What are you doing in Paris? he asks her.

Visiting a sick friend, she says. She inhales from her cigarette. She needs to quit smoking, she thinks for the third time that day.

I'm sorry, the man replies.

It's okay, she says. It'll be, you know, fine.

The man senses she really doesn't want to talk. He decides to ask her his question. Is there a closer Metro stop than Pont de Alma? he asks. I'm visiting a friend and we're supposed to meet at five and I was just wondering 'cause that stop isn't so close and with this weather and all.

She looks above his head. I don't think so, she replies. I think that's the closest. I'm being short with him, she thinks. I didn't sleep much last night. I'm allowed to be short.

Thanks anyway, the man says.

No problem, she says. What's your name? she decides to add.

Adam, the man replies.

The woman laughs. I'm Eve, she says.

Wow, he says. How funny. How often does that happen?

Right, Eve says.

Paris is the closest I've gotten to paradise, he says, so maybe it's no coincidence.

Eve smiles. Do you like New York? she says.

It's the center of the world, he tells her, and he really means it. What do you do in New York?

I write plays, she says.

I design costumes, he says.

No one does my plays, she says.

No one wears my costumes, he says.

I'm so tired of this, they both think at the same time.

Well, he says, if anyone ever does your plays, I'd be happy to clothe your actors.

Sounds good, she says. At this point in her life, she is convinced no one will ever produce her plays. She has applied to graduate school but doesn't feel like bringing it up, especially to a stranger. She isn't excited or happy about the prospect of going back to school. She feels like she's failed.

A policeman runs by Eve and Adam. Adam hears the word *coeur* over the policeman's walkie-talkie. Heart. He cannot make out the rest and figures even if he could, he doesn't remember enough French from college to understand what it means.

Do you like the heart? he asks her.

She hesitates. She wants to say something profound but cannot think of what to say. It's big, she finally tells him.

He is surprised by her answer. But he knows she wants him to leave. He stares at her red lips and says, It is. I think it's pretty neat.

No one says neat, she thinks. She gets a chill. It is still drizzling. She looks up into her umbrella.

He looks at his watch. It is 4:19. Time to go, he thinks. Thanks for the help, he tells her.

I didn't help you, she answers.

Thanks anyway, he says.

Maybe I'll see you back home, she says.

Maybe, he replies. He says good-bye and turns to walk away. A man with a Polaroid camera and emerald eyes gets Adam's attention. The man is dressed in all black, a black tank top and black pants. He has a tattoo of a snake wrapped around a sword on his upper right arm. He must be a model, Adam thinks. I wish I looked like that. Adam walks by him and stares. The man does not look at Adam.

The man with the Polaroid camera gets Eve's attention as he walks by her. She watches him pass. She is strangely and suddenly fascinated by the man. She looks at her watch. She has ten minutes until she has to meet her friend. She figures what the hell and follows the man with the camera and the snake tattoo.

Adam turns around to see Eve and her red umbrella walking in the opposite direction, toward the esplanade. He wonders where she is going. He has an urge to follow her, but his thoughts are interrupted by a rapidly approaching siren. Adam spins around to see a small ambulance drive off the road and onto the pedestrian area. People scatter and leave a wide space for the ambulance to drive through. Adam watches as the ambulance proceeds down this path toward the tower, underneath, and finally to one of the legs. The leg with the open stairwell in it.

Some people follow the ambulance. Some people go back to their business. After some consideration, Adam decides to follow neither Eve nor the ambulance. He heads for the Metro.

A man in a brown suit sees a younger American-looking man quickly walking away from the tower. Easy, this man thinks. He briskly approaches the younger man and bumps into him. Excuse me, the man in brown says. Sorry, the younger man replies. The younger man, a little flustered, continues his walk. The man in brown walks back toward the tower with the younger man's wallet in his hand. He passes a sign that says BEWARE OF PICKPOCKETS in both French and English.

No one pickpockets anymore, a tourist from Canada thinks as he reads the weathered sign. Honey, let's go, he says to his wife, who is carrying their beige umbrella. Don't call me honey, she thinks but doesn't say anything as usual. They walk toward the esplanade. The wife sees a crowd has formed near an ambulance at the left leg if you're looking out toward the esplanade. She wants to see what's going on, but she knows her husband is in a hurry to get to their next destination. He's always in a hurry, she thinks. Even on this vacation.

There are fifteen German tourists in the crowd around the ambulance. One of them, a tall man dressed in a Nike jumpsuit, understands someone has had a heart attack while attempting to climb the stairs. The stairwell has now been closed off and the French paramedics are trying to figure out the safest way to get the man down. The German man is thanking god it is not he who has had a heart attack. More and more people gather to investigate.

A small Scottish woman leaves the crowd. She walks toward the esplanade. Poor man, she thinks. Poor, poor man. What a horrid day, she thinks. Someone holding a lily walks by. Don't hold lilies if it doesn't really feel like spring, the Scottish woman thinks. So what if the months say it is spring. It doesn't feel like it. She sets her eyes on a man holding a dog on a leash. It's too cold for a dog to be out! the Scottish woman thinks. Take him in!

Stupid dog, the man holding the leash thinks. The dog runs to a passerby. The passerby stops to pet the black dog. The black dog licks the passerby's hand. You can have him, the man holding the leash thinks.

Gross, the American woman petting the dog thinks.

The dog spots a woman holding an umbrella. It's a red umbrella, except it appears only black and white to the dog. She looks like everyone else to the dog. It doesn't occur to the dog that the woman with the umbrella is looking at a man with a snake tattoo and a Polaroid camera.

The man with the Polaroid camera stops near a tree on the esplanade. He turns around and sees a woman holding a red umbrella and standing at the edge of the pavement. She might be nice in my picture, he thinks. She might be. Her umbrella would be nice, at least, he thinks. With the tower in the background, the heart and the umbrella would complement each other perfectly. He notices that she keeps glancing at him. She thinks he doesn't know. He knows. He wonders what she is thinking.

The woman with the red umbrella wonders why this man is taking pictures with a Polaroid. She suddenly remembers a dream she had last night. It was actually a dream within a dream. She was in a rain forest and someone took a picture of her next to a waterfall. A few moments later, she woke up and realized she was dreaming. She turned to look at the clock on her nightstand and saw a picture of her with the waterfall next to the clock. She tried to grab the picture. Then she truly woke up.

As she watches the man with the Polaroid point his camera in different directions, she thinks, What if we could take pictures of our dreams? What if there were a way to document the visions we have while we sleep? Maybe we could know ourselves better and, in turn, better ourselves if we had pictures of our subconscious. If we knew our deepest thoughts, the thoughts that won't come out during the day, perhaps we could know all there is to know. Before she can form her next thought, the man calls to her.

Move in front of the tower! he yells to her in English.

She points to herself as if to say, Me?

Yes, he answers. Move in front of the tower!

She looks at the tower. She moves to where she thinks front would be. Is this right? she yells back.

He looks though the viewfinder. Perfect, he calls to her. He pushes the button and a picture pops out of the front of the camera.

Anything else? she calls, hoping somewhat that he'll say yes.

What time is it? he says.

She looks at her red watch. Four twenty-nine, she tells him. She remembers she has to meet her friend.

Thanks, he says. For the picture and the time.

Okay, she answers. She sees him flapping the picture upside-down in the air. He is not interested in her anymore. She has many questions to ask him. She wants to know his thoughts. She wants to know what the picture looks like. She hesitates and then turns around and walks toward the tower, where she is scheduled to meet her friend in thirty-nine seconds.

The man with the Polaroid and the tattoo stops waving the picture. He watches the red umbrella as it moves farther and farther away from him. He looks at the picture he has just taken.

The sky is gray, almost purple. It is raining. Drizzling. The usual numbers of people are milling about around and below the Eiffel Tower. Some people line up underneath to buy tickets to go to the top. The people who are not waiting to ascend the great tower are looking up at it. Some people are carrying lilies. The grass in the esplanade in front of the tower is green and the trees there are becoming green. There is a beautiful woman holding a red umbrella in the foreground. There is a crowd of people gathered around an ambulance at the right leg of the tower in the background. The Eiffel Tower looks the same as it always has, except for one thing. On the top of the iron structure, a large red heart has seemingly been impaled there.

Listen.

I don't want you to think I'm some sort of Birkinstocked pantheist when I tell you this, but it's true: My kitchen table had amazing powers of prophesy. Now, I don't "do" metaphysical. My chakras are unaligned, my past lives unregressed, I've never consulted a psychic. I don't even do yoga, okay? But this is different. It's eerie how the tiles on that table mimicked and mocked us, foretelling the demise of Jack's and my relationship. It was a gorgeous table, though. Dark grayish-brown wood, rough-hewn, pitted and scarred, and in each corner a crazy-looking Mexican tile showing the four seasons depicted by those *Día de los Muertos* skeleton people.

Jack and I had decided to keep my apartment instead of his because not only was he living in the same building that David Koresh grew up in and the karma was just too freaky, but my apartment had the huge balcony, the off-street parking, the funky coffeehouse next door. Besides, Jack was in Colorado for two months and I wanted to suck the last bits of marrow out of my life as a single person.

All that June I'd sit in the kitchen; blue rag rug from Pier One covering the stains on the floor where the home brew experiment went wrong, kick-ass Lynda Barry cartoon taped to the refrigerator, my beautiful dishes with the fish on them sitting out on the counter because they were so gorgeous they deserved to be looked at all the time. There I'd sit, elbows propped on that table, which would chain me to this town, this house, this man for the rest of my life, and I'd make lists. Thirty-five days until Jack comes home. That's three paychecks. That's fifteen pounds. That's five more times I can watch *Melrose Place* without his making fun of me. Thirty-five days can be my lifetime.

Then the phone rang. Jack.

"I didn't know Outward Bound lets you make phone calls."

"I'm sick. Really sick. Pick me up at the airport at 9:35, okay? Delta."

Here's where I'd like to say I first realized the psychic powers of the table, but I'd be lying. The winter skeleton didn't move in his tile, his bony little face laughing as the snows fell. My eye didn't fall on him as I was grabbing my car keys. I didn't suddenly Know. I just threw my lists away, fetched Jack from the airport, and took it from there.

This isn't a story about Jack's illness. I don't want to talk about the trips to the hospital, the weird stains in the bathtub, the sound of Jack gasping in the kitchen as I tried to sleep. Instead I'll let the pictures on those Mexican tiles tell you about his recovery.

Now, I've always been a Dexatrim-and-cigarettes-for-breakfast kind of girl. Jack was the big health nut in our house; buying salads at Wendy's, that sort of thing. So it was no surprise when, a few weeks into it, I came home to find him sitting in the kitchen staring into the open refrigerator.

"Why do you buy this shit?" he asked. "No wonder we're sick."

"I'm not sick," I said.

"Yeah, but you're not healthy. Look at yourself. Jesus. We need to eat better."

So we went down to Whole Foods and bought our bible: *Zen Health, Zen Sex, Zen Longevity,* by Jason West. We went home, fished a couple of Rolling Rocks out of the vegetable crisper, and sat down to read. We skipped the Longevity section. I wanted to go right to Sex, but Jack insisted on reading the Health part first.

Zen Health, Zen Sex, Zen Longevity is a sweet little book, full of chapter headings like "Wanted for Murder: Killer Milk" and "Follow the Meat Eaters to Their Early Graves." We loved this book. Every day we read, embraced, and implemented a new chapter. Jack would read it aloud to me in bed in the mornings. It was kind of erotic, like reading *The Story of O* or something. And the kitchen became our playground, our battlefield. Lynda Barry had to share her space with charts of which foods are yin and which are yang. The black and white counter-top sprouted juicers and slicers and a bread-baking machine that we only used once. The vegetable colander took up permanent residence in the sink. The summer skeletons danced and sang. This was their perfect hour. Teamwork, consideration, a common goal. Lots and lots of sex. They knew that this was as good as it could get. So what happened? What changed?

We were following the book to the letter. I lost weight. Jack got better. Life was golden. Then Jack bought another book. *Fasting,* by a Professor Eichmann. I didn't trust a man who wouldn't tell me his first name. Besides, I've read *Mademoiselle.* I've read *Cosmopolitan.* I know what happens to girls who fast. For the first time in my life I was getting in shape, and now Jack was trying to tempt me into an eating disorder. No way.

In bed. Thursday morning. It's raining outside. I wake Jack up. Since he's stopped eating animal products he won't go down on me anymore, but I figure it can't hurt a girl to try. As he kisses me, Jack murmurs, "Professor Eichmann once went forty-nine days without eating anything." Jack is getting hard. "When he's not fasting, Professor Eichmann only eats once a day." He pushes into me. "He won't eat any foods that digest into mucus." Jack times his thrusts with each word. "He only eats fruits—" BAM! "—and—" OOH! "—nuts," WHAM! "He's called a . . . a . . . a . . . frugavore!" As he says this final word, Jack comes. Hard. He rolls off me and lies back, eyes glazed, mouth slack. "Frugavore," he repeats, reaching down to touch himself lightly.

That day I go to the Crossroads Market and buy a book of feminist erotica, which I read in the kitchen as Jack reads the fasting book in the bedroom. The skeletons are on Jack's side now. For them and for him it is springtime and life is full of rich possibility. The trees are budding. Jack rips the scary-looking portrait of Professor Eichmann out of the middle of the book and tapes it up on my refrigerator. I rip it down. He in turn rips down Lynda Barry. I cry. He goes into the bathroom and locks the door. Many days pass like this.

I sit at the table and make a list of all the positive things in my life. Um. My mind is blank. Start small. I can drive a stick shift. I can recite "The Wasteland" from memory. I bet I'll get into the master's program at Rice. I'm in charge of my life. I can choose my destiny. I can do anything I want. To hell with Jack, I'm moving out.

Then I look at the table.

The skeletons look back, make some eye contact, grin. I don't move out.

I buy a two-liter bottle of Coke. Jack won't let me keep it in the refrigerator because he thinks toxins will escape from the plastic and circulate, contaminating his organic plums and pears.

I start to eat meat again. Ice cream, pretzels, frozen waffles.

After a while Jack's good health starts to catch up with him. He was fasting four, five, six days at a stretch. His skin turned a funny shade of yellow, he started walking into walls, and he developed a constant tic under his right eye. Then one day he fainted while driving down Montrose Avenue and plowed his Jeep into the side of a taqueria. He called me to come pick him up at the police station.

I bring along a bucket of chicken, which I set on the chair between us while we wait for his paperwork to be processed. Jack can't take his eyes off it.

"I drove by your old apartment," I tell him. "It doesn't look like it's been rented yet."

Jack's still looking at the chicken. "That's disgusting. I can't believe you're eating that. Don't you care about yourself at all?"

I pat his skinny yellow arm. "Why don't we give your old landlord a call? I bet he'd take you back."

Jack very gingerly picks up the bucket by one edge and peers inside. "Unbelievable," he says. "Chicken. It's just too much."

Later that night. Jack's throwing his stuff into boxes, loading them into the back of my car. I go into the kitchen to wait. We haven't discussed who gets custody of the table. The autumn skeletons are the only ones left. Everything is dying, falling, growing cold. I turn my back on them and look around.

These are my beautiful plates, I think. This is my black and white countertop. The skeletons scream, brutal, desperate. I open the drawers and cabinets. These are my forks and knives. Green glass candlesticks. Coffee mug. Corkscrew.

THE WHITE CAROUSEL HORSE   Dennis G. Dillingham, Jr.

She preferred the white one. A princess, she knew, rode a white horse, not a pink one, a purple one, or a blue one. There was no reality in any of those. She had a sense of reality when it came to horses, the color of them and the associations made between color and things such as woman and man, girl and boy, good and evil. That sense is what kept her from the darker colors too: a child's sense of associative realities. Or maybe she simply preferred the white one.

It had been much whiter, now nearing an off-white, an age-stained version of something that was once as white as the clouds or a sun-bleached cement walk. And its hooves must've been much blacker once, and its mane much blacker. They revealed now a weakness in the animal in those places where the paint had chipped away, leaving grayish, clay-colored spots, the discoloration a parent associates with illness. That beautiful, once-white horse was suffering from a pox and no child ought go too close. Stay away from that horse, ride one of the others. The pink one is clean and healthy. Why don't you ride the pink horse instead.

She knew it wasn't sick. She knew it was pretending so the other children would stay away. The white horse was faking illness so that only she would dare climb up onto its saddle. That was the way she liked it.

Somewhere along the way, the carousel operator, the strange old man with the gray poet's beard and a pocket full of lollipops, had been replaced by a button, a small, red dot, an eye, that a different and grim-lipped man would, when a satisfactory number of saddles had been filled and a sip had been taken from the flat, silver flask he kept hidden inside the lapel of his green workman's jacket, press on his way to apathetically cleaning out one of the over-pouring garbage pails, leaving the keys that controlled it inserted and unattended. That, too, was the way she liked it.

Privacy, she liked her privacy, and though an occasional lollipop would have been appreciated, this was better. Nothing to scare the horses or the clouds or to eat the music before it reached her and her stallion's ears. They both relied on the carousel music, and the two would ride all day as long as the music played, but when it stopped . . .

She didn't like it when the music stopped. That was when her horse rested, sometimes resting all through the night, forcing her to go home and dream about him instead. But her dreams never seemed to get it right. The music was always a little too slow or the whiteness of the horse a little too bright, sometimes a little too dark, and then there were the other noises; and the other noises were loud, sometimes drowning out the music entirely. Even in her dreams, she couldn't stop her horse from resting.

The other noises scared it, the raised voices on the other side of the wall, where her parents slept, the shouting and the pleading and, sometimes, the shattering of things ceramic or glass or porcelain—it all sounded the same when broken. And some nights, there was the slamming of doors and the sudden rattle of the car starting in the driveway, and then, eventually, the car returning, the creak of doors being opened slowly and with deliberate care, the whispering her thin bedroom walls could never stop and then nothing but the ringing silence. The other noises scared it and, though she knew very little about horses, she knew they wouldn't run when they were frightened, or maybe they would run too fast.

She would lie awake at night, many nights, eye-tracing the shape of her horse on the dark ceiling above, wishing the crease of moonlight that squeezed through her tightly drawn blinds would dance the way her carousel lights danced: over her head and under and around, laughing and singing, and not simply fall lazily on the foot of her too-long bed. She would lie awake many nights, determined to get the speed of the music right in her dreams but struggled to hear even the simplest note over the other noises the night awoke. Fighting to hear the too-slow carousel music, she would drift off to sleep, her horse resting, the lights extinguished, and the music consumed by the noises the walls could never stop.

Some days her mother took her to see her horse and would sit on a bench nearby watching her go around and around and around. Her mother would sit all day, for as long as she wanted to ride. Her mother would sit and watch and smile. Or maybe, it only seemed like a smile, maybe it was an illusion. She was spinning fast, her horse carrying her so swiftly around the park that anything could have been stretched into a smile. From *her* eyes, though, it was a smile.

When she was done, or when it was time for her horse to rest, she would walk over to her mother and, every time, or at least every time she was now able to remember, her mother's eyes were wet and the skin underneath red and soft like the nose of her heavily breathing stallion. She would think to ask her mother if she had been crying, because she knew crying too. In the way she knew the realities of color, she knew crying. She remembered when she first experienced it, the tingle turning to stinging, the movement down her cheek like a summer-fly slowly exploring the surface of her face. It was when the noises started, the other noises, the wall-noises that scared her horse at night. The noises that kept him from running, that kept her from playing the carousel song in her dreams, that kept her room as loud as it was dark. She didn't know if she could play it before the wall-noises, before her parents stopped bringing her to see her horse together, before they stopped bringing peanut butter sandwiches and fruit. She didn't remember very much before then, before the first of the slowly pacing summer-flies came to her cheek. She imagined that she could play it, though, and sometimes that thought made the summer-flies swarm until her pillow was damp with them, and sometimes it kept them away.

She would think to ask her mother if she had been crying, but then, remembering the discomfort of the summer-flies, would ask if it had rained while she was under the carousel roof. Her mother would smile, nearly laugh, take her hand, and the two of them would walk home. As they walked, she would tell her mother about her day riding, about the jumps her horse managed with ease, about the trees and the flowers she had seen along the way; she would tell her about the music and the lights and how when you got going fast some looked like stars and others looked like fireflies that came so close to your nose you had to be careful not to breathe them in, and still others looked like fairies. She would tell her mother all this and the softness beneath her eyes would harden. And wiping the remaining wetness from her face, her mother would smile and tell her to hurry, pulling her gently, saying they weren't to get home too late.

On other days, her father took her to see her horse. He wouldn't sit on a bench like her mother, but would stand beside the carousel platform. He would never smile but would only watch her with a distance to his eyes, looking almost beyond her. After a short time, he would tell her she had enough and that it was time to go home. It was never enough when he said it was; she always wanted to ride more, ride farther, keep riding. Sometimes she thought she wanted to ride forever, and just as this possibility occurred to her, he would take her stiffly by the arm and they would go home together, neither of them smiling.

Other times, when the desire to continue riding overcame her, she would tug against his grip, trying to get back to her horse. His fingers were always too firm. And when she began to cry, he would, without fail, release his fingers and apologize, crouch down, his eyes glassy and red, take her softly in his arms, and tell her that everything was going to be all right, everything, he would tell her, was going to be all right. She never understood what he meant. To her, nothing seemed all right; she was leaving the park, leaving her horse before he had to rest, but she knew it was best to smile, take his hand, and not mention the pain in her arm.

After days like that, she returned home and struggled even harder to keep the figure of the horse firmly placed on the ceiling. She would even try to convince the thin crease of moonlight to dance, and, desperately, she would try to play the carousel song over the wall-noises, but never could. And instead of any of this, instead of the horse or the dancing light or the music, the flies would visit her, and she liked the flies least of all.

The other noises soon became louder, stealing some of the brightness from the now even narrower crease of moonlight and eating more of the music. She slept less, no longer able to find the solace the prospect of morning had once provided her, the prospect of again climbing onto the back of her beautiful boy and riding until all she felt was the rhythmic motion, the wind against her face, tossing her hair with its gentle fingers: the sheer joy and contentment she once found there. But soon, as the noises grew, these feelings lessened and sleep became more difficult; everything she had associated with her horse was slowly being replaced, forgotten.

She cried more often now. She cried because she was unable to enjoy her horse as she once had and she cried because she knew that she could never enjoy it as long as the noises ate the music from her dreams.

Soon the flies stopped, replaced with the rain that softened the skin beneath her mother's eyes. It was then that she decided.

She sneaked from the dark and dreamless room, through the house, the sounds of her steps swallowed by the noises, and out into the cool autumn night. The moon was only a sliver, a sly grin no wider than the crease that fell each night on the foot of her bed, but it was deeper and free, surrounded by nothing but space. She immediately noticed the freedom the moon had and began to feel sorry for the crease, sorry it was forced to be in the room with her where no dreams could ever live instead of at home in the deep, cool night sky, where, she imagined, dreams could live with ease, flying about without the fear of ever being swallowed. It was unfair, she thought, as she moved through the grass of the front yard, the rubber toes of her sneakers collecting the dew the night had labored to place on each individual blade. The lawn was glazed sublimely and glistened like the surface of a lake at sunrise as the sparse moonlight danced off each drop of condensed night air, but with each step, she unintentionally erased the night's efforts.

She made her way through the yard quickly and stepped onto the dull and hard asphalt without hesitation and continued, leaving wet prints behind with each step. She was making her way to the carousel.

The park was less than a mile from her house, and, once in the street, she began to walk with urgency. She didn't know what she was going to do when she got there. She hoped she would see the lights dancing and she hoped she could hear the music at its proper speed, but more than anything else, she wanted to see her horse, her beautiful white stallion.

She walked, and her thoughts were kept from the pain in her heels as they landed on the unyielding asphalt with each heavy step, and were kept from the weariness in her legs and her eyes by the thought of climbing onto his back. Tonight she would ride longer and farther than she ever had before, forever maybe. Tonight would be the night she wouldn't return, she thought, and she began to run.

Soon she was at the park's gate. There were no lights, but determined, she proceeded into the darkness, amid which she could hear nothing but the pounding of her own heart, her breath, which had become exaggerated in the much cooler night air, and the crickets that were singing so loudly she thought a few had nested on the lobes of her ears. The carousel was there, standing in front of her, darker than she had ever seen it. She stood a moment, surrounded by the sound of her heart, her breath, and the crickets, staring at the dark, still, and quiet carousel. She couldn't even make out the colors of the horses and wondered how she would find the white one. Slowly, she moved closer.

The colors became more visible as she neared the carousel, which now, standing just before her, seemed to loom lifelessly in its dark silence. She hesitated, startled by the image, but then she saw him, beautiful and white. He was awake and waiting for her. He knew she would come for him, to free him, she thought. She wouldn't abandon him the way she had the crease of moonlight, she would help him break free.

She leapt onto the platform, began stroking his mane, and whispered in his ear.

"There's my boy," she whispered softly. "There's my boy."

Eagerly, she climbed up onto his back and, taking care not to kick him, placed her feet into the gold stirrups, leaned forward, and laid her cheek flush against the black hair of her horse's head, which was even cooler than the night's air. She was cold. She hadn't thought to bring a jacket or a sweater, but her horse would keep her warm, she thought. He would protect her.

She sat with her head resting on his for some time, but it soon became too dark, too quiet, and too cold; they both knew it. She lifted her head and scanned the darkness until she found it: the little red eye, the button. She could see it across the platform, luminously red in the darkness, nestled in a booth behind a wire gate, noticing the keys that hung just beneath it as only a distant shimmer in the night and nothing more.

She dismounted slowly, deliberate with each movement, and wove her way in and around the other horses, who were all sleeping. They were quiet and dreaming, she thought, happy and dreaming in the colors of their coats. That was the difference between her stallion and the rest, and she was going to free him from it all.

She made her way across the platform to the tiny booth that held the eye of the carousel, but the gate was locked. She reached her hand through a gap in the gate, but her arms were too short and the button too far away for her to reach it. She began to cry, but then her eyes caught on something off in the grass. It shone in sharp contrast to the surrounding black, seeming to catch a bit of the night's light and tossing it in her direction. She ran to it. It was a long silver stick, the kind the man used to poke garbage with. She grabbed it, sprinted back to the platform, and struggled to reach the button again.

She tried, but she still couldn't reach it. Behind her, one of the pink horses was quietly sleeping, and without a moment's hesitation, she climbed up onto its back. She knew her horse wouldn't mind her mounting one of the bright ones for the sake of their freedom, but with her feet in the stirrups and sitting in the saddle she was still too short.

Her parents told her repeatedly never to stand on the horses. It was too dangerous, they preached emphatically, she might fall and hurt herself. But they weren't there, and she knew she couldn't let her horse remain trapped, like everything was in the room with the noises. No, she wouldn't let that happen, and using the horse's head for support, she carefully placed her right foot onto the saddle, followed by her left.

Her sneakers, still wet from the grass, slipped slightly on the horse's saddle, but she recovered and took a moment to ensure her balance on the animal. Once certain of her footing, she reached the pole between a gap in the gate and, with a hard jab, poked at the red button, missed, steadied herself on the horse's back, and jabbed again. This time she connected with the button, and, suddenly, the carousel came screaming to life.

The blast of music and light startled the pink horse and it bucked, sending her crashing onto the hard carousel platform. The music was playing and all the horses were awake now and running. It was playing at the right speed and it seemed to completely eat up the sounds of the crickets, her heart, and her breath.

She tried to stand, but her leg hurt and it stung when she tried to move it. Across the platform, she saw her horse running without her. She yelled for it to wait, but it wouldn't. It kept running and she yelled again, but by now it was galloping away from her. Frantic, she began to drag herself across the platform, between the other horses, and toward her own.

She got to her horse and put her right hand around one of the stirrups, which shimmered like actual gold in the light. She pulled on it, reached up and grabbed the edge of the saddle, and managed, while fighting back tears, to position herself on her horse's back.

They rode together with the music chasing the crickets from her ears and filling the cavernous night sky. The lights were dancing all around her, above and below, swooping down and up and back. She was surrounded by fireflies that danced and landed on her nose, took off and landed again, and on her eyelashes sat the fairies. She didn't swat at them like she might a cricket or a summer-fly, no, she let them land wherever they wanted and would let them stay as long as her horse kept running.

They galloped together, and she told her horse about the other noises and how she had escaped but how she had to leave the crease of moonlight behind. Her horse just smiled and galloped along gracefully. She told him how they were going to run forever and never look back and how nothing was ever going to eat the carousel music again. But as they galloped, the music began to disappear, slowly, note by note, it began to fade, replaced by other less-melodic noises. Then a dissonance resembling the wall-noises began to fill her ears, and, from the corner of her eye, she saw two small, round lights off toward the entrance of the park.

As she rode, the lights grew larger and the noises louder and more defined, clearly, now, voices. But she ignored it, put her head down, and whispered to her horse to keep running.

"Don't stop," she whispered. "Keep running."

FIRST SNOW

That fall and on into winter it was a joke among the other five of us on our roadside crew, something we'd say to cement the bonds between one another and keep Maurice safely outside our little circle. Colin, who was in for robbery, and who was, at twenty-three, the oldest of us, and by far the most clever, came up with the catchphrase.

One morning Maurice had said, as we rode in the back of the van on our way to a cleanup site, "Take one step toward Allah and he'll take two steps toward you." When he spoke, we could never be sure if he was directing his words at us or talking to himself, so quiet was his voice, his gaze always set off to the side or down at his feet. The rest of us looked around at each other, sneering at this bit of wisdom so early in the day. In us an anger still simmered. Now I know it; it's the anger of those who have been on the inside for only a couple of months, the anger of incredulity that someone would dare to take you away from your life and put you behind a twenty-foot barbed-wire fence. We were white; we were young; we were angry. Allah was as much our friend as the cops who had taken us in.

For three hours that morning we picked up trash and rehearsed what we knew of proud silences and defiant expressions. Once or twice a car zoomed past with a girl inside, dark hair whipping in the wind, still parading a summer tan in her bikini top even though by then it was late September and cold in Michigan, and we shouted after her and gave chase for a giddy half-second before Greider, the guard, brought us to a stop by raising up his club. We had no doubt that he'd use it. Maurice worked on his own, a little bit away from us.

At noon we ate sandwiches in the back of the van; Greider dozed up front with a newspaper over his face, a curtain of wire mesh and Plexiglas dividing us. I don't know if Colin had spent the entire morning cooking this up or if he divined it in that moment, but once he'd finished his lunch, he entertained himself by faking sudden hard punches at Maurice. At each feigned blow Maurice flinched and seemed to draw back further into himself; he was so mute and withdrawn it was hard to tell when Colin spoke whether Maurice was ignoring him or simply didn't hear. "Hey, guys, I got one for you," Colin said, looking around and gathering his audience the way he always did before delivering a line he knew we would prize. "Check it out, you take one step toward Maurice, he takes two steps *away* from you."

We all laughed; maybe I laughed the loudest, I don't know. The laughter of men on the inside is sad and cruel. Joyous laughter, exuberance, exhilaration; these had no place in our lives at Galloway Lake Detention Center. I've been in a lot of other places in the years since and some of them were a lot worse, dangerous, completely devoid of humor in any form; in some prisons I have also seen, on occasion, a bright twinkle in the eyes of some of the older guys that bordered on real merriment, but it was always followed with the same wistful and lost look. Every emotion can basically be experienced in two distinct ways: as felt in freedom, and as felt in shackles. There is happiness behind bars, but it is always chained to something large and immovable. Anger, on the inside, has no place to go. Even loneliness, and grief, and loss, cannot be felt as fully in prison as when you are free.

At least for the five of us, targeting Maurice, laughing at his expense, suspended the monotony of our rage. The little quick breaths that came with our snickering seemed to relieve for a moment the pressure mounting inside us. We spent six mornings and afternoons a week along one sixteen-mile stretch of I-94, roaming the high dry median weeds and the steep marshy embankments, picking up refuse, items so unwanted and vile that highway motorists couldn't bear to keep them in their cars until they reached a trash can at home. We filled hundreds of blue plastic bags with fast-food wrappers and diapers, pop cans rattling with bees, jagged debris left from high-speed collisions; weeks passed and still the joke had not lost its luster. "Take one step toward Maurice," Justin or Nick or John Jay might say once we were back in the back of the van with the bags of garbage we'd collected that day, and we'd all crack up before they even finished. Maurice would stare ahead as if he was trying to fade into nothing. Sometimes he'd turn away. The joke gave a rhythm and shape to our days.

Galloway Lake was not really even a prison so much as a small work camp for first- and second-time serious offenders. For me, and for most of us, it was our first time inside, so when the air got colder, and the leaves changed to yellow and orange and red then to brown and at last detached themselves and fell away, and we knew winter was on its way, a certain desperation latched onto our hearts. It's a peculiar sensation, that first change of seasons when you're locked up. You begin to understand that while time is frozen for you, it continues on for the rest of the world. Pain constricts your insides. There's an inescapable heat and ache at your temples. It becomes hard to breathe. I know all of us felt it because our attacks on Maurice came with renewed viciousness and vigor. We never laid a hand on him— Greider's presence prevented that—but we spat abuse in his face. I remember Nick was the most relentless. Nick told me once that I was. Through it all, I knew that Maurice had been chosen as our victim not only because he was black, and different from us in countless other ways, but because he was the weakest, and weakness, above all things, could not be tolerated. It is no defense, but I offer it as a fact: had I been the weakest, they would have preyed on me.

Maurice, though, Maurice was exceptionally weak. He was just a few inches over five feet, so slight as to resemble a child. He wore big glasses that he cleaned every few minutes by rubbing spit on the thick lenses before drying them with a fold of his pant leg. Some guys retained a quiet dignity in backing away from confrontation. You had the sense that everything you said to them went unnoticed. Maurice, on the other hand, seemed to exist in a state of constant fear and agitation. He trembled at our approach. Insults stung him visibly. The only reason he did not retaliate was because he was so afraid.

Thanksgiving passed, a cold holiday. We missed the turkey dinner because our van ran out of gas a mile from Galloway Lake and Greider had to radio for another van. December came, and with it gray skies and even colder days. Colin said that when it got too cold they'd take us off highway cleanup and put us to work in the kitchen or the laundry room, but all they did was issue us warmer outfits and gloves. In the colder weather there was less trash, since tossing things to the roadside required people first to roll down their windows. Sometimes we'd stretch out in a wide semicircle, Maurice off to the side a little, Greider watching us from the shoulder. We'd talk about football and girls we used to know, our eyes flickering over the flashes of passing traffic. I recall thinking once that to the people speeding by, on their way to school or work in the morning, or in the late afternoon heading home to their families, we must have appeared to be roadside garbage ourselves, littered across patches of grass where no person would ever think to rest. Now I doubt anyone noticed us.

It was one week before Christmas. Cauldrons in our chests were ready to boil over. The morning was flat and dull gray and bitterly cold, and as we picked our way along the edge of the road toward the blank billboard at Exit 150 that always marked the end of one segment of cleanup, it began, without warning or fanfare, to snow. Fat, heavy flakes swept around us. We acknowledged this development wordlessly and kept on, crouching to scoop up a brown paper grocery bag, or to grasp the long black rubber snake of a blown-out tire. Hot diamonds of snow burned at my cheeks like tears, and I rubbed them away before they could melt.

At last we climbed into the back of the van for lunch, and it was then, with the winter's first snow touching softly against the back windows, in the silence created by our disbelief and our madness at the sight of it, that Maurice, face buried in his hands, began to moan a little. He let out a sudden choked sob, and then, to our horror, sat up and began to speak to us, blurry-eyed and disoriented.

"None of y'all prob'ly give a shit about me, I know that," he began, and I looked up at John Jay, expecting him to tell Maurice he was right, but John Jay, and the rest of them, were frozen by his voice. "Last night," he went on, "news came, they got me up outta my bunk." Then he paused and squeezed his eyes tight against some thought. Again, I waited for someone to interrupt him, to tell him he would not be heard; I didn't know what he was working toward, but I wanted desperately for him to be quieted. "See, my brother, he ain't mixed up in nothing. Now that's a good kid." Maurice's voice had a shaky, tremulous quality to it. After every few words he took in a deep, staggered breath and then nodded to himself and forged on. "My brother got good marks. My brother worked up at the . . . at the . . . up at Norton Pharmacy in the summertime. My brother, he come an' visit me every week, every Thursday, soon as he get off school. My brother, he run track, too. He run them hurdles, he run the relay. Carl Lewis, that's what I call him. I say, 'Carl Lewis, you break the school record this week?' I say, 'Carl Lewis, you hittin' the books like I told you?' Kid always had a head on his shoulders. Kid was like a math genius. He ain't ever done dirt, I made him promise me that. I told him, 'Carl Lewis, you ain't ever comin' in here like me.' Kid had his shit together. Had himself a nice girl." Maurice teetered to one side like he was about to topple over, then righted himself. He took off his glasses, spit into his right hand, dabbed the thumb of his left hand into the saliva, and worked it in slow, tiny circles at the lenses. We must have watched him for five minutes. My head was clouded. A hot emotion flooded me. I felt the blood push sluggishly through my body. Up front, barely audible, was Greider's country music. A thick white blanket formed over the back windows.

Maurice seemed to have collected himself, but after he had dried his glasses on his pants with numbed difficulty and replaced them over his eyes, he began all at once to cry. "Chaplain come last night an' told me. What happened is, what he says is, what he told me, chaplain said, 'Your brother's dead.'" He wailed at the sound of his own voice presenting the information. "He got done in. Never meant no one no harm, but they done him in on accident, gunnin' for Marquis Eddy next door." Now he was really hysterical, but not a one of us moved or spoke. I was dead inside. Blackness filled me, a bolt of nausea. Something in my core threatened to break apart and I strained to keep it intact. Maurice cried harder, and he kept crying things out. "I can't go see him," he gasped, gripping his head with his baby hands, still sitting straight. "I just want to see him but they puttin' him in the ground. They puttin' him in the ground. They puttin' him underground."

"Shut the fuck up," I heard someone say slowly and evenly, and then I realized the voice was mine. Maurice kept on, and I said it again, a space between each word as though they were four separate commands. "Shut—the—fuck—up!"

But by that point he was beyond us in his misery. He cried on for his brother and for himself. "I want to go home," he wailed. "I want to go home. I want to see my brother. They're puttin' him in the ground. It's snowing. God! It's snowing!" Tears and snot clung to his upper lip.

The van started up at that moment and Greider swung us up onto the road; the back end slid a little in the fresh snow. We drove for three minutes to another spot. Maurice whimpered and struggled for breath. As Greider came around the back of the van to let us out, I shouted at Maurice so loud it shook him from his stupor. "You!" The breath caught in his throat. His eyes came into focus. "Now shut the fuck up," I told him.

What happened next is a little hard to piece together because it was so unexpected and because it all happened so fast. First the back doors swung open and I saw Greider plainly against the falling snow, a hard, balding man of fifty years, thirty of which he'd spent in Corrections. "Okay, everyone out," he said. He never bore resentment toward any of us as long as we made his job easy and behaved. I didn't really know him. Days later, in the aftermath of what followed, I met his wife and his children and his grandchildren.

The car that hit him seemed to come from nowhere. One moment the road behind Greider was empty, and the next a wide black Buick was flying sideways at all of us. It struck Greider and then the van. The impact tossed us in a heap on the floor. I remember next only that we were all standing outside the van—Colin, Nick, Justin, John Jay, Maurice, and I—and that Greider was crumpled in the snow like a flattened pop can, and that the Buick's tires were spinning like mad on the shoulder. The tires finally grabbed the pavement, and the Buick shot away and disappeared into the curtain of whiteness. Already, snow had begun to accumulate over Greider's legs, his back, and his arms.

The six of us stared dumbly at one another. Here it was, a chance for escape. The keys had burrowed a place in the snow a few inches from Greider's hand. We could be miles away before anyone even knew what had happened. But our time at Galloway Lake was nearly half over. Running made no sense. They would catch us again, and this time they'd keep us in for longer. In our minds then, we had only a few months to go, and then we would be free.

Had Maurice remained silent, the next part of it might have gone differently. "My glasses," he said to nobody, groping blindly toward the ground. "Where are my glasses?" John Jay turned toward him and made this odd sound, a kind of low and disapproving hum, and launched himself at Maurice, ramming him with his forearm and shoulder. Maurice crashed to the earth and lay there stunned for half a second, staring up into the blank sky, before John Jay landed on him, flailing his fists, crying, "Stupid nigger, stupid nigger, stupid nigger." Then all of us were around Maurice, dragging and carrying him behind the side of the van, out of sight of the infrequent passing cars. He never raised a hand up in defense; he never had the chance. Two of us held Maurice by his shoulders up against the van while we took turns battering him. We hit him with our elbows and with our fists. We kicked at him. We spit on him and shouted things. All the while the snow fell. Giant snowflakes stuck in our hair. Maurice's blood was pink on our hands and on our uniforms; the madness of it brought great wild smiles to our faces. We danced and sang. It seemed as if our whole lives had been lived in preparation for this celebration. We beat Maurice savagely, with pride, with glory.

After a long, long time, we had expended ourselves. We stood apart from each other. Maurice lay bloodied and broken, halfway beneath the van. John Jay stared out toward the bare trees of the birch woods before us. Nick caught snowflakes on his outstretched palm. Justin watched the road. Presently, Colin broke away and went over to Greider's motionless form. "Hey, guys," Colin said vacantly, "he's pretty bad messed up. We better get him to a hospital." John Jay grunted in agreement and the two of them lifted Greider gently into the back of the van. He was still breathing. John Jay climbed in beside him and tried to comfort him. Nick and Justin joined John Jay. I sorted through the spiny ball of keys for the one to the driver's door, got in up front, and reached over to unlock the far side for Colin. He got in, and then, as an afterthought, we both got out and pulled Maurice from under the van and put him in back with the others. I started the van, crossed the eastbound lanes, bumped over the grassy median, and headed west, toward Jackson and the hospital there, into the snowstorm.

Already, my mind had recoiled from the beating. It occurred to me in my daze, as I leaned forward in the seat, flipped on the lights and the wipers, and fought to keep the van from fishtailing while still driving as quickly as I could, that just a few hours ago it had been autumn—late autumn, but not yet winter—and that now it was winter. I became dimly aware that although I would be freed in the spring, it would not be long before I was locked up again, and that realization hurt me worse than anything. I knew also that the only way I could have avoided this future of a lifetime of incarceration was if, immediately after the accident, we had grouped up and gone for help, or if right away we had attempted escape. Escape would have been impossible, but flight would have substituted itself for what had just transpired—that terrible release—which I could not in that moment, or for many years, remember.

THE CARNIVAL

Clementyne Howard

At this carnival there was no popcorn. There were no games, no prizes, and no children. There were no laughs, or music, and there were no merry-go-rounds. At this carnival, there was only a bunch of clowns—a bunch of people grouped together in the same white place, all hiding under the same painted-on faces.

As I walked into the carnival, I was filled with nervous tension. My body was shaking and I was chewing so fiercely on my bubble gum that my jaw began to ache. I signed in and the lady who was behind the counter said to me, "Okay, Miss Ross, if you will just have a seat right over there until we call your name." The lady was not one of the clowns. She simply worked for the carnival. She got to wear normal clothing—nice black pants and a white blouse with red designs around the collar. She wore a colorful pin that read HAPPY HOLI-DAYS. She seemed calm and detached, and her emotionless coun-tenance clashed with the rest of the characters in the room. I guess she was used to the scene, and was used to leaving her emotions at home.

Everyone else in the room was waiting there for the same reason. We were all experiencing a common fear, and we all wanted this expe-rience to be over so that hopefully we would all be able to go home and take off these ridiculous costumes. I bet everyone there regretted the circumstances that brought them to the carnival. We were all clowns to end up there in the first place.

The walls in this place were white and the chairs were red. In large black letters a sign read FREE TESTING. There was cheap artwork adorning the wall next to the counter. There was a wooden rack that stood upright containing brochures with titles like "Help for the Needle Abuser" and "Making Sex Safer."

To my left a man and a woman sat together holding hands. He was the clown wearing one of those "joke" flower pens—the kind that is actually a squirt gun that fires out black ink—and she was the clown with the sparkled hair. Did she know that the flower was really filled with ink? And how much longer would he continue to think of it as only a joke?

In the corner was a man standing on stilts, looking more confident than the rest of the people in the room. He had one of those large red smiles painted on his face. He had dark black paint around his eyes, and white paint covered the rest of his face. It looked as if he had spent a long time creating his facade. It looked as though he thought his stilts made him stronger than anyone else in the room. They called his name—"Mitchell . . . Mr. Mitchell"—and he followed a lady dressed in white through a door and down the hallway. The door shut hard and the man was gone.

The room was quiet except for occasional, brief conversations. I could periodically hear questions asked to the lady at the counter like, "What time is it?" and "Do you know how much longer I'll have to wait?" The clowns were becoming impatient. I was becoming impatient. I bounced my leg viciously on the floor and I could feel it shaking my chair and the one next to me. My curly yellow wig was beginning to feel too tight. I desperately wanted to pull it off of my head and throw it into the trash can, but I had to keep it on—it was part of my punishment for being part of the carnival.

I saw one of the clowns, whose name had been called earlier, walk out of the door that led to the doctor's offices and back into the waiting room. She looked like she was probably in her mid-twenties and she had large red hair and was wearing a dress with polka dots on it.

She had been carrying red balloons earlier, but I guess she left them in the doctor's quarter. She was grinning slightly, and by the look on her face I could tell that she had heard good news. She walked past me and gave me a consoling, sympathetic look. I watched as she pushed her way out of the large, heavy glass door and as she got outside she stopped by the trash can. She pulled the red wig off of her head. She removed the rubber band from her hair. Her long, dark curls caught the sunlight and dropped gracefully onto her shoulders. She tore off her ugly, oversized dress. She had on a brown skirt and blazer. She then balled up the red hair and the dress and shoved them deep into the trash can. Before she got into her car, she looked back at me through the glass as if to once again show me her compassion, then stepped into her black Camry and drove away. She was glad to leave the carnival.

I envied her. I wanted to be the one who could leave and smile and put the carnival behind me. I wanted these nauseating feelings of intense dread to end. I sat there for what seemed like a painful eternity and suddenly the door to the doctor's offices swung open and slammed against the wall. Four ladies dressed in white carried the man who had been on stilts through the door. He was crying and wailing and fighting them. His black face paint was running over his cheeks and onto his clothes. The red paint around his mouth was still there, but his mouth was wide open. They carried him across the room and through a set of unmarked doors that I had not seen previously. He was in a state of undescribable agony. Would it be me, too, that they would carry across the room screaming? Would the carnival reduce me to a pile of fake yellow hair and rubber shoes?

I sat there still, silenced, and shocked, as did all of the others. A minute later a fifth lady in white walked through the door carrying the man's stilts. One was broken. She carried them across the room and through the unmarked doors. Following her, a lady came out and said my name—"Ross . . . Miss Ross." I did not want to move. I was too scared. I did not want to be like the man on the stilts. I wished that I hadn't been forced to come to this carnival. I wished that I was not a stupid clown. "Is there a Miss Ross here?" said the lady. I sighed and then answered—"Yes . . . I'm here"—and I walked toward her. I heard the door shut loud behind me. As I walked down the hall, one of my big red shoes fell off. I wondered if that was a good sign.

PETTY THEFT

Martin Wilson

From up the aisle, where he was hanging packages of press-on nails on a rack, Cary saw a girl holding a brassy tube of lipstick between her thumb and index finger, as if it were a precious vial of something she needed to inspect closely to appreciate. And he was still watching her when she tucked it down the front of her shirt into her bra. He had seen this particular girl at the store before—always around three in the afternoon, after the schools let out—roaming the aisles, playing with her stringy, damaged-looking blond hair. He figured she was sixteen, perhaps a sophomore or a junior in high school somewhere in town. On those scattered days, he had never seen her actually buy anything, but he didn't follow her every move, so it was possible she did sometimes pick out things and pay for them.

But now he had seen her steal, which may have explained why she always left—when Cary observed her—empty-handed. The girl continued down the aisle, oblivious to him. He saw the white straps of her bra creeping out from under a black tank top that didn't cover her flat midriff. She wore torn jeans that barely hung on her hips, and her face was painted with heavy black eyeliner and hot magenta lipstick. It was not a look that suited her dainty figure, her fragile-looking face—it was forced, like a costume.

Cary stopped hanging the press-ons and thought about what he should do. Mr. Haynes, the manager of the store, had told him on his first day that he should always report any suspicions of shoplifting right away. "It's not usually a problem in this branch," Mr. Haynes had said, referring to the more affluent area of town where the drugstore—called Harco—was located. "But you never know."

Cary thought about hightailing it to Mr. Haynes's little office in the back and telling him. But then he pictured the awful scene that might follow: the girl denying it and then screaming, acting belligerent, crying and begging them not to call the cops, she'd give it back, please don't have her arrested. The awkwardness of it all. Cary didn't want that kind of drama; he hated shouting and all of that attention-drawing humiliation. All for a tube of lipstick.

Still, he stood on the verge of doing something, of telling someone, but then decided to let it go, the moment passing as quickly as it formed. He turned back to hanging the pretty, fragile fingernails, in shades of red, purple, even gold and silver, long and short, ridiculous things he couldn't imagine anyone wanting to go to the trouble of using. But he couldn't focus now, and he turned and saw the girl rounding the aisle, moving deeper into the store. He wondered how she could walk so calmly with that lipstick tube firm and cold against her slight breast.

Cary had been working at Harco for about five weeks. The store was one of many locally owned branches in town, and so far it had withstood competition from the larger, national chains. This particular branch was only a mile from his mother's condo, where he was now living. He considered it a temporary job, a way to keep busy and make some money until he was ready to go back to the university and continue his degree. It was the perfect job for him, he thought, because it offered a variety of unstressful duties: stocking shelves, unloading boxes, serving as a cashier, taking film development orders, occasional mopping, a little creative product display designing.

But what he liked best about the job was that sometimes he got to assist the pharmacist, Mr. Laskin. Laskin was pasty and quiet and always donned a scowl. He wore thick-lensed glasses and slicked back his thin brown hair with water and petroleum jelly. Cary suspected that Laskin was a drunk, because he often came in smelling of vodka and Scope. From Laskin, Cary learned which pills accomplished what—Niacin for blood circulation, Claritin to help with allergies, Ritalin to calm the hyper kids, Tetracycline for acne, and countless other pills whose names all started to blend in one big medicinal lexicon of healing. Usually, while Laskin took his lunch, Cary was able to sneak pain pills—Vicodin, Lortab, Lorcet, Darrocet, and mostly Valium. He was careful in his stealing—never too many at once, never the same pill too many times in a row. The pills gave him a soothing high, made him less anxious about things he wanted to forget about— kind of like being drunk, but less sloppy, more in control, numb and peaceful. Pretty white pills that were petite but potent.

Before he took the job, and before he took a sabbatical from school, he had been sidetracked by what his mother had called a "slight nervous breakdown." But he wasn't so sure that's what it was at all. To Cary, a nervous breakdown was when people went completely nuts and had to be committed someplace until they got their head screwed on tight again. A nervous breakdown was romantic—it meant sitting in some hospital or New Age resort, listening to classical music, wearing white gowns, and being carted in a wheelchair through lush gardens while sipping pink lemonade. Cary didn't feel as if he had gone off the deep end or anything like that—he was as sane as anyone else was. No, what happened to Cary was that he just refused to leave his apartment for almost two weeks, until his mother had her boyfriend, Wes, kick in his door and drag him out. When asked why he had done it, he couldn't explain it to them, to anyone—why he had holed up for a week, closed off from the world, eating just cereal and crackers, sipping from lukewarm soda bottles. Something had made him want to stay put, to just lie still and not move—some unnamable, misty feeling of fatigue. If he had tried to explain it, they wouldn't have understood. His mother said his little breakdown was just stress-related, and Wes said it was because of his lack of exercise and his poor diet. The shrink—whom his mother had made him see, but only once—accused him, in a subtle and uncombative way, of doing it for attention. If they needed explanations, then Cary was happy to just let them think what they wanted to think.

But this job at Harco, it was good for him—a definite step in the right direction. It got him up out of bed, gave him some kind of purpose, made the time go quicker. Plus, he had people to talk to, to exchange views on the world with—things he missed after he had left school, especially since he had lost touch with most of his college friends. And he had access to the pills, of course. He had never taken drugs before this, had never really even drunk much in college, but he had heard one of the girls at work talk about how great the Valiums were when she had dislocated her shoulder. How the pain just vanished, how it made her float a few feet above the world. It got Cary thinking, and there they were, the Valiums and others like it, all sitting about in large jars, so many of them, and this was a local store, the ship wasn't run so tightly—he could get away with it. A few pills, no big deal. They wouldn't be missed—just like the tube of lipstick the girl had stolen. Petty theft.

When he got off work around five, Cary went straight home. His mother's condo was in a gated community named Wellington Estates, a community filled with divorced middle-aged men and women, a few widows and widowers, and some of the wealthier and quiet-seeking young upstarts in town. His mother liked it there—the tennis courts, the clubhouse where she could go for drinks and bridge games, the roving security personnel in their black shirts and black shorts.

Cary, however, still missed the house he had grown up in. After the divorce, his father moved to Texas and left him and his mother alone in the big house. His father was in the oil business, a petroleum engineer, and the divorce settlement was cushy, leaving Cary and his mother nicely cared for. But his mother didn't like the house and its mammoth size, mainly because there were so many floors to mop, surfaces to dust, light bulbs to replace. The thick, bright-as-a-golf-putting-green lawn was maintained by a team of three gardeners who came each Monday, and she hated having to supervise them. The house and everything connected with it, she decided, was too much.

When Cary came in from work that day, his mother was doing abdominal exercises in front of the television in the living room. She wore black Spandex shorts and a tight hot pink Lycra tank top. He still found it funny seeing his mother wearing such tight, youngish garb, but she had a nice figure for a woman her age, and at least she didn't wear such things out in public like some less shapely mothers he had seen.

"Hey, honey, want to join me?" she asked. "I have this great fifteen-minute routine, really gets the abs tight and burning."

"No thanks." Just after the divorce his mother had turned to weightlifting and exercise; she told Cary that she was going to "fight flab," that her new goal in life was to remain firm without the aid of plastic surgery. "I'm not going to be like those other women," she said. So she joined the Muscle Planet Gym, and this is where she met Wes, who was a trainer there. Cary held Wes in awe: His arm muscles were as sculpted and hard as plastic, his shoulders broad and solid as a podium, and his face was as chiseled as that of a comic book superhero's. After weeks of workout flirtations, Wes and Cary's mother started dating, and Wes eventually moved into the condo.

His mother, crunching away, letting out quiet squeaky grunts, started to ask him something, but he dodged her by charging up the stairs. He wanted a pill, deserved one after his day. His room, before he moved in, had been the guest room, and it had been done up in whites and ivories, fluffy pillows all over the bed, heavy drapes over the window, and not a personal memento anywhere. But he had altered it a bit since then. He stacked the pillows in the closet, and he covered the floors with his books and magazines, which he only really looked at or skimmed, never read. He had put his small TV on the nightstand, but he usually only watched it with the sound on mute. And his clothes—

the select few he wore now, like his khakis, his worn gray T-shirt, his Harco uniform shirts—hung next to his mother's off-season outfits. The rest of his belongings were in storage, hidden away in cardboard boxes.

He opened the nightstand and pulled out a brown-tinted vitamin-C bottle. This is where he kept his stash of pills, and he was running low, just a few tablets rattling around inside. He shook one of the pills into his hand and walked downstairs to the kitchen, poured himself a glass of water, and swallowed it.

"We're having shrimp kabobs tonight," his mother shouted from the living room. Cary joined her there, awaiting the calm that was soon to set in. "Wes is outside grilling," she said between crunches.

Cary plopped down on the couch, watched her, watched the local news, which only seemed to report awful things—today a baby had been scalded by hot soup, the baby-sitter arrested.

"How was work?" she asked.

"Fine. The same."

Wes came in through the French door that led out back to the small brick porch and the tiny backyard with a lawn the size of a picnic blanket. "Howdy, Cary. Dinner's almost ready." He was wearing walking shorts that couldn't help but hug his hips and butt tightly, a wrinkly Polo shirt, sandals. He carried a tray of the grill-pinkened shrimp, charred green peppers, shiny slivers of onion, all impaled artfully on the little kabob skewers.

Cary liked Wes. At first he tried to dislike him, as if it was his duty to hate him—the new, other man. But he was so likable, always smiling, goofy enough to seem pleasantly stupid, and even though he sometimes pressured Cary to pump iron or hit the treadmill with him, Cary could tell it was out of concern and not because he was one of those obnoxious spread-the-glory exercisers. Besides, Wes was good for his mother. She looked younger now (her eyes less bloodshot, her hair kept youthfully long), woke up earlier in the day, and though she had no job, she seemed more productive. Wes's energy was now his mother's energy.

His mother pulled herself off the floor. She looked at Cary. "What's wrong—you seem weird."

"Nothing's wrong. I feel fine."

"You can always quit the job, you know, if it gets to be too much for you," she said.

"It's not too much for me, for Christ's sake."

She half-smiled back at him and nodded.

"Well, I'll make the salad and then we're ready," Wes said, pinching his mother on the ass, hustling her into the kitchen. Cary just sat on the couch, didn't feel like moving. He closed his eyes and could see the girl from the store at her home, putting on that lipstick, licking her lips, smiling, kissing the mirror, feeling charged because she had gotten away with it.

"Dinner's ready, Cary!" his mother shouted a few minutes later.

But he wasn't hungry.

When the girl came in the next day, Cary was at the front cash register with Dale, one of his coworkers, who was always telling him about his girlfriend who had gone away to college and how he missed her but did she really expect him to never look at or maybe even date another girl? Dale had receding red-brown hair and his face was scarred with long-gone acne, but he had nice gray eyes and a bulging Adam's apple and Cary could see how a girl might want him. Dale was probably his best friend in the store, but they had never done anything socially—they hadn't crossed that boundary yet, and Cary doubted they ever would.

When he saw the girl glide in—hands in her pockets, eyes off in their own world, still wearing those jeans with the suggestive, jaggedly ripped holes, and a shirt that was unevenly buttoned—he was glad she had shown up. She ducked down the Easter candy aisle.

"Can you cover this register for me for a minute?" Cary asked, interrupting Dale.

"Well, I mean—"

"Only for a few seconds. I've got to go to the bathroom."

Before Dale could respond Cary walked off, ducking down the same aisle, past the yellow-boxed chocolate bunnies and the purple and pink bags of cream eggs and jelly beans. He found the girl in the cosmetics section, a shimmering lane of plastic compacts and brushes, a rainbow of rouges, and pictures of shiny, happy-faced beauties on the boxes, enticing the women customers to buy this or that. He hid behind a stand of tanning products and watched her. What today? Perhaps some nail-polish remover, or some skin-toned zit cream? She seemed more cautious, maybe aware that someone was watching her. It took her about five minutes before she edged—easily, because her pants were so loose fitting—a package of peach-colored blush down the front of her jeans. She didn't even look around.

Cary stepped out from behind the stand and approached her, as if he had just happened to round the corner. She had her eyes focused on sparkly nail polish when he asked her, "Finding what you need, ma'am?"

"Yes," she said. She didn't act nervous or surprised, just sounded annoyed.

Cary looked at her, at her jeans where she hid the blush.

"What are you looking at?" she said. She looked angry, her eyes scrunched up and her mouth stretched tightly, but then she smiled a fake beauty pageant smile and stuck out her tongue, then curled it back in slowly like a carpet being rolled up. She turned back to the shelves, glanced back at Cary, who stood and watched her as if in a trance. "Jesus. What is your deal? I'm leaving," she said. "This is harassment."

He almost said something to her—"Give it back," "I saw you," "I know what you did"—but she had walked away by the time he'd summoned the courage.

Cary chased after her, slowly, and saw her walk out the door. He went to the door and watched her walk, self-consciously yet very gracefully, across the parking lot. She sat on the hood of her cherry-red Honda and took out the blush and opened it and spread it all over her face with the brush, as if she were carefully painting a ceramic egg. Even from a distance he could see her face—freakishly orange around the cheeks. It made her look like she had suffered second-degree burns.

He stood there for some time and watched, until Dale came up to him, his breath on his neck. He smelled of cinnamon Tic-Tacs. "You want her, don't you?" he said, giving a little chuckle.

"No, not at all. It's just—"

But he couldn't tell Dale. He couldn't rat on her. He looked back and saw her take out a cigarette and struggle lighting it.

"That's what I need," Dale said. "A young thing like that."

Cary almost protested again—that he wasn't sex-crazed or any-thing—but instead went back to the counter. Dale, still at the door, said, "She's staring over here. I think she wants me."

"I'm sure," Cary said.

The next time the girl came in the store she was with her mother, a woman Cary not only recognized but knew. And when he saw the two of them together, he realized that he had seen the girl before he had ever worked in Harco. The girl's mother was Jackie Higgins, a woman his mother used to play tennis with, before the divorce, when she still had her club membership. Jackie Higgins and her family also went to the same Episcopal church, though Cary and his mother had stopped going there months ago, too. The club, church—these were just some of the many things that fell away from their life after his father left, like little pebbles following a boulder in an avalanche.

The Higgins girl. No wonder he hadn't recognized her on her vis-its to Harco. At church she had looked completely different: She always wore her hair in a ponytail, had on little makeup, and her clothes were pastel in color, schoolgirlishly cute. Today, a Sunday, she looked very much the same way, but Cary was still able to recognize her, her moody eyes. Her hair was done up in these ridiculous braids—it looked like an elaborate pastry was glued to the back of her head. She wore a baby blue dress, so it was obvious they had come to the store straight from church. Cary had just finished setting out an Easter display in the small front window of the store, filling it with plastic grass, hollowed-out sugar eggs with tiny, blissful scenes inside, and plush bunny rabbits with oddly evil grins on their faces. But he stopped what he was doing, climbed out of the window, and walked up to Mrs. Higgins and the girl, who avoided looking at him. "Mrs. Higgins?"

"Oh, hi. How are you today?" she said. She picked up a blue plastic shopping basket. He could tell by her blank face that she didn't know him.

"I'm Cary Dinsmore, Loraine Dinsmore's son? From St. Luke's Episcopal?"

"Oh, yes, good to see you. . . . Yes," she said. "Loraine, of course." She looked at his shirt uniform and his acrylic name tag. "How is she? Is she still dating that bodybuilder?"

"Yes. She's fine." He was surprised she knew about Wes.

She nodded. "So, you work here?"

"Yes, ma'am," he answered, though they both knew it was a dumb question meant to fill conversation.

"Well, that's great."

Cary had often seen his mother's old friends in the store, and when they were confronted with the knowledge of his employment there, they usually acted overenthusiastic about it or were at a loss for words. It never bothered Cary, really. He was not ashamed of his job. Mrs. Higgins sounded much the same way as those women did.

The girl, standing off to the side, scratched her shoulders, which were buried under the stiff dress that seemed too big for her. Cary thought she looked ridiculous in it, unstylish and awkward, like a baby doll in human clothing.

"Listen, where are your tennis balls?" Mrs. Higgins asked. "I think y'all have moved things around on me."

Cary led her to the proper aisle and out of the corner of his eye he saw the girl veer toward the cosmetics aisle, her usual haunt. Mrs. Higgins squeezed the airtight cans of tennis balls.

"Where did Louise run off to?" Mrs. Higgins said, not shifting her eyes from the plastic cans.

So, her name was Louise. Louise Higgins.

Mrs. Higgins rolled her eyes. "I bet she's in the makeup section. That girl and her makeup. Her father and I limit the amount she can wear." She picked up another can and squeezed. "But I know she buys it and puts it on at school."

Mrs. Higgins had unknowingly offered a small glimpse of Louise's home life. Strict, it sounded like. A house that forced Louise to sneak around. He imagined she had been forced to go to church, too.

"Well, I appreciate your help," Mrs. Higgins said.

It took Cary a minute to figure out that Mrs. Higgins was telling him, nicely, to leave her alone. But before he walked off, Louise rounded the corner, still scratching her shoulders. She locked eyes with Cary. Mrs. Higgins's back was to Louise, so she wasn't yet aware that her daughter had walked up. And maybe Cary imagined what happened next, but when Louise grinned at him—tilted, cocky—he thought that she was letting him know that she was fully aware that he was onto her and that she knew he would never do anything about it. It was as if she knew about the pills, about Cary's breakdown, about his father.

Cary ran out of pills a few days later, and he spent that night tossing around in his bed, falling in and out of odd, obnoxious dreams, finally waking up at five because peaceful sleep was impossible, apparently. That next day while he was unloading new magazines at Harco, he tried to figure out when he could snag a new stash. He usually took the pills at lunch, but he hadn't assisted Laskin for a few days and found no excuse to be back in the pharmacy. The next best time to steal them was whenever he worked at night, when the pharmacy was closed, when he could fix it so that he would be the only worker at the back counter near closing time. But he hardly ever had to work at night and wasn't scheduled to do so for another few days. He began to think that he wouldn't be able to pull it off anymore. He tried not to panic—after all, he didn't need them.

When he looked up from the crate of new magazines, Louise stood before him, staring at him. He didn't know how long she had been there.

"Hi, Louise," he said.

She looked away, fast, like he had scared her. She fiddled with her hair and walked back to her favorite aisle. Cary didn't follow her immediately, but finished unpacking the glossy magazines that all smelled of expensive perfume.

When he found Louise, she was fingering bottles of shampoo, big bottles that she couldn't possibly place on her body inconspicuously. He walked up to her this time, instead of waiting to catch her in a steal. "Hi, Louise, I'm Cary. Our mothers know each other. Remember?"

"I don't remember you," she said. She moved away from him, swung her hair out of her face.

He followed. "How's your mother?"

She grasped another bottle of shampoo and held it in her hand like a phone, close to her ear. "What?"

"How are you?"

"Leave me alone," she said. She turned away, still holding the bottle.

"Okay," he said. He let out an awkward, nervous laugh and stood where he was. "I've seen you steal, you know."

She made no expression but instead opened the bottle and sniffed inside. "This smells like cow piss," she said and made a gagging face.

"I could report you if I wanted."

"I don't know what you're talking about. Now would you let me shop in peace? I'll complain to the manager if you don't stop."

"Okay," he said again, and this time he walked back to the magazine rack, though he'd already finished placing them on the shelves. He tried to interest himself in the cover tag lines because his heart was pounding: "Six Things NOT to Say During a Breakup," "What She Wants to Hear After Sex," "How to Say You're Sorry—Again." He wondered who wrote such articles, who led such lives that they could proffer advice like this. Didn't they have problems? How had they come by their wisdom? He wanted to snatch them all up—women's and men's magazines, it didn't matter—and read like crazy, to see if anything in there really could help. Then he heard sneakers squishing closer and he looked up. Louise shuffled past him, out the door. She carried a green bottle of Pert shampoo in one hand and shot Cary the bird with the other.

At home that night Cary was tense and restless. He had not been able to steal any pills, after all. He was sitting on the floor of his room when Wes knocked and came in.

"Hey, Champ, your mom said to get ready for dinner."

Cary nodded at him. He realized he was still wearing his Harco uniform, which was just a crimson red shirt top tucked into khaki pants, with the name tag pinned over his heart.

"We're going out to the new Italian place by the river."

Cary just nodded again.

"You okay?" Wes asked, coming farther into the room, pulling out the desk chair and sitting down.

It was Wes who "rescued" Cary from his lock-in stupor all those months back. His mother had apparently sent him over to check on him. Cary remembered Wes's repeated knocking followed by the explosion of the door nearly falling off of its hinges. Very cinematic of Wes. Wes later said that Cary was lying on the floor next to the couch with a thick literature anthology lying open next to an empty box of tissues, the carpet littered with crumbs. After talking to Cary, trying to rouse him, Wes picked him up from the ground and carried him like a bride over the threshold and took him to the condo. His mom had started crying when

Wes plopped him down on the bed in the guest room—his room now—and left them alone. The next day, after sleeping on it, she would blame his little incident on stress, but that night, wiping her eyes with her thumbs, she said, "It's all my fault, isn't it? It is."

"Cary?" Wes asked again. He had leaned forward in the chair and was waving his hand in front of Cary.

"Oh, sorry. Yeah, I'll be ready in a minute."

Wes walked out of his room cautiously, as if at any moment Cary might have some sort of seizure. When he was gone, Cary pulled open the drawer again and took out the Vitamin-C bottle, shook it to confirm that it was, in fact, empty. He still hadn't changed shirts or moved from the floor when he heard his mother shout from downstairs, "Cary, are you ready?"

At work the next day he had to rearrange some shelves, replenishing stock where needed, filling up the blank spots, making things look full and bountiful, that sort of thing. Dale was helping him, but Cary really didn't listen to what Dale was saying, because he kept hoping to find a way to get to the pharmacy. But the opportunity never presented itself. In the afternoon, still at the same duty, he started looking for Louise, but the afternoon faded into evening and she never showed up. But ten minutes before he got off from work, Mrs. Higgins appeared. Cary was making room for packages of Q-tips when he saw her walking toward him. She carried a brown paper sack.

"How are you?" she said.

He nodded and was about to make pleasant chat, but she didn't let him. "I need to talk with you. Do you have a moment?"

"I get off in about five minutes."

"Perfect. I'll wait outside for you." She smiled weakly at him—it was more like a quick tensing up of her lips than a smile—and walked away.

After he filled out his time sheet and said his good-byes, he walked outside and found her waiting by a newspaper dispenser. He noticed for the first time that she was in her tennis skirt and a jacket, wearing a visor even though the sun was rendered red-pink behind the evening clouds. She suggested they go over to her car—a Volvo station wagon—but they didn't sit inside, just stood by it.

"What can I do for you?" he asked, as if they were in the store still and she needed assistance.

"Well, Louise talks about you all the time. She says very nice things about you."

His throat was dry. "What does she say?" he asked.

"Well, Cary, that's what I wanted to talk to you about. You see, Louise says you give her things from the store. Because you like her, she says."

"I give her things?"

She nodded her head and gave him that anemic smile again. "See, she no longer gets an allowance from me or her father—she only wasted it, and we thought she needed to learn a lesson about money, that it doesn't grow on trees, you know. Louise said she told you all this at the store?"

"Of course," Cary said, stunned. It was like he had walked into a movie theater and the movie was already halfway through and he couldn't follow things. He almost turned to try to find someone who could explain it all to him. Rush-hour car horn honks started at the intersection at the end of the parking lot.

She continued: "Well, even after we stopped giving her money, she always brought things back with her. She tried to hide it at first, but I must admit I snooped in her bathroom and found all of this, this *stuff*." She laughed and shrugged her shoulders, but Cary knew she wasn't really feeling guilty about snooping; he could tell she thought it was her right as a parent. "So I asked her how she got those things, and she told me they were gifts, from you. She said you felt sorry for her, having no money. She called you 'that nice tall boy with the tired-looking eyes.' I knew immediately who she was talking about."

"I think you've got this all wrong."

But she was too wrapped up in her own story and ignored him. "Now, Cary, as much as I appreciate getting presents and as much as I appreciate someone being so kind to my daughter, these gifts really should stop. I don't think it's healthy, really. A grown man giving gifts to a teenage girl?"

Cary had never heard himself referred to as a "grown man." It rattled him. He paused a few minutes and said, "There's been some misunderstanding, Mrs. Higgins. You see . . . I mean, Louise steals those things." He didn't look up to see her expression. "I let her do it, I see her do it, and for some reason I haven't stopped her."

"Steals?"

"Yes, ma'am, she steals. I don't want her to get in any trouble. Louise has a problem, I guess, but—"

"No, no—*you're* the one with the problem," she said. She fiddled with her visor, situating it better on her head, took a deep breath, and seemed hesitant in what she was about to say. "I know about you, Cary. Everyone always refers to you as that Dinsmore boy. Loraine and John's son."

Cary wanted to find his car and drive away, or maybe go back into the comfort of the store. But he couldn't help picturing people at dinner tables, talking about him, pitying him, some maybe laughing at him. He pictured Jackie and her tennis partners, trading volleys at the net, laughing and talking about the "poor Dinsmore boy," so depressed, so nuts, so broken up about his father and his slutty mother who drove the man away. Once a bright kid, that Dinsmore boy, now a college dropout, stocking shelves at Harco. Suddenly, Cary felt sick to his stomach. And he ached, ached for a pill. He wanted to float away from this place.

"I sympathize with you, Cary, I do. I understand your problems, and I sincerely hope you work through them one day. You can't help it, considering certain things." She gave him a knowing glance. "But please, don't start making silly accusations about my daughter." Her tone had shifted from phony concern to real, tentative anger. "I wanted to give this back to you." She handed him the paper bag she had been carrying. "I tolerated your giving gifts to Louise, at first. But with this you went a bit too far."

He looked into the bag and saw a white box. He pulled it out and looked at it for a moment, at the pink and blue writing, the cropped picture of a man holding a woman, both of them smiling. Even after he read the product name—Easy Step—it took him a few moments to register that this was a home pregnancy kit. He quickly jammed it back in the bag. He couldn't look at Mrs. Higgins now, so he just stared at his shoes. But he could feel her peering at him, and all he could think about was Louise having sex with some pimpled boy or Louise having sex with Dale in the back alley. He looked up. "I don't know what's going on here," he said. "Louise steals those things. She shoves these things down her shirt. I've seen her. And one day she's going to get caught." He said this all without raising his voice.

"I see, and you let her do this, you *let* her steal? No. Listen, please stop giving Louise gifts, or I'll have to talk to your manager."

"Talk to Louise," he said. "You need to talk to her," he said.

Jackie opened up her car door and got in, smoothed her skirt out, fastened her seat belt, ready to shut the door and drive away.

"She dresses like a tramp. How can you let her look that way?" he said, walking to her door and resting his hand on it so she couldn't close it. "Mrs. Higgins, she steals those things."

"Take your hand off the door."

"She steals." His voice was still quiet; he felt choked.

"Get some help."

He moved his hand and she slammed the door. But before she drove off, she rolled down the window. "If Louise brings home one more of these gifts, I'm talking to your manager."

After she was gone he stood there for a minute, with the bag clutched to his chest. He dropped it on the ground and found his way to his car. On the drive home he felt as if someone had lurched up out of the dark and slapped him a good one. It was the same kind of feeling he had gotten when his father had left him a note on his bed a few years back, explaining that he had found work in Texas and had to leave right away, to settle in. An empty, stunned sort of anger, with a sort of powerlessness about it. The worst thing was that his father left while Cary was working as a youth counselor at the Episcopal church camp, where the kids drank wine coolers and smoked clove cigarettes and some even had oral sex down by the creek. He had hated it, the responsibilities, the kids he was supposed to counsel—all of them surly and spoiled. Being a counselor had been his mother's idea—it will look good on your resume, she said, it will show leadership. But all he did there was get bitten by mosquitoes and read scripture, sing a few songs, and drink cheap beer smuggled in by one of the other counselors.

When Cary got home from camp after two weeks, dropped off by the church-owned bus, his mother met him at the door and hugged him, smothered him. His father and mother had been having problems—arguing over how she spent money, how he worked too much, how she flirted like it was a sport; through the years they'd always fought and made up, but as they, and Cary, got older, the fights grew in number and the apologies shrank. Sometimes Cary found it hard to believe they'd ever been in love enough to have a child.

Of course, the camp gig was a way for them to get Cary away from home while they dealt with the sticky, logistical divorce details, which they'd finally decided on. So when he saw his mother at the door the night of his return, he somehow knew then that his father was gone. He walked, slowly, to his room and found the note. It was written on a piece of a grocery bag, in a felt-tip pen, the scrawl barely legible. Just a note about Texas, his new start, where he promised Cary could visit. Soon. While he read it—over and over again, all seven lines of it—his mother told him that his father had wanted to visit him at camp, to explain things.

"But I told him he shouldn't," she explained.

"You did, huh?" he said, but he could barely speak much more than those few words because he was choking. He had so many words he wanted to shout at her right then.

His mother hugged him from behind, and he stood rigid. Then he felt her begin to cry and shake, and her tears started wetting the back of his shirt. Eventually she pulled away, sniffling.

"See, I knew he would just upset you, and I wanted you to have a good time before you came home." She went on and on, and only stopped when Cary climbed under his covers and started shouting, finally, into his pillow.

After he got home from Harco, Cary sat in his room the whole night, claiming he had a stomachache. His mother brought him Pepsi and crackers but mostly left him alone. He fell asleep with his clothes on and woke up while it was still dark out. He wasn't set to work until the afternoon, but he showered that morning, put back on his uniform, and went to Harco anyway.

When Cary entered the store, he saw Dale unloading packages of gum at the candy stand below the front counters.

"What are you doing here?" Dale said, glancing up, then back down again, as if unloading gum required his full attention. "You don't work until later."

"I just wanted to stop by." Before Dale could respond, Cary felt a tap on his shoulder and turned to see Mr. Haynes.

"I didn't expect you until the evening, Cary."

"Yeah, I know." Cary smiled. "I didn't have anything to do, so I thought I'd drop by to see if you needed me."

Dale stood up and walked off with the empty gum box without saying a word.

"Well, I'm glad you're here now," Mr. Haynes said. He was wearing a light blue long-sleeved shirt with a too-short brown tie, a pocket protector empty of any pens, and his tiny glasses that made him look benevolent, like Benjamin Franklin. A kind man. Cary wanted to hug him.

"I'd like to talk with you in my office."

"Sure," Cary said.

"Well, why don't we go on back."

When Cary sat down in the back office—just as he had months ago when Mr. Haynes interviewed him—Cary all of a sudden felt that everything was wrong, especially when Mr. Haynes shut the door behind him. He was no longer a calming presence, but a threatening one. Had Mrs. Higgins already called him as she had threatened? Cary sat there with a chilled dread rising up in him.

Mr. Haynes wasted no time, offered no cushioning buildup to what he was about to say. "Cary, I know you've been stealing pills."

Cary was silent but he looked Mr. Haynes in the eye. "It's not my shift right now, as I said, but I could mop up if you want. The floors look sort of dirty," he said.

"Laskin did inventory last week and noticed them missing. Now, we began questioning employees and, well, someone has said that they saw you actually doing it. Stealing the pills. Do you want to deny it?"

Cary just sat there. Dale, it was Dale who told—he was sure.

"Are you in trouble, Cary? Are you okay?"

"What?" he said, still trying to process what was happening.

"Cary, I'm afraid I'm going to have to let you go."

On Mr. Haynes's desk the picture frames were all turned down. It was unbelievable, Cary thought. Why have pictures and not look at them? Cary picked up a brass frame. In it was a photo of a heavy woman in a blue dress, perhaps Mr. Haynes's wife or sister. She held a white rabbit, a real one, and a carrot. She stood in front of a church and she was squinting because it was sunny.

"Nice picture," Cary said, watching the woman's features blur in his shaking hands.

"I'm not going to involve the police in this, Cary. Laskin wanted to press charges, but I said I wanted to talk to you. Cary?"

"Has the rabbit died yet? Because the rabbit my dad got me for Easter one year died. A neighborhood dog got it. Mom said it was a lousy gift—the rabbit. I guess she was right," he said, letting out a short laugh.

Mr. Haynes cleared his throat, an unpleasant noise. "Cary, I think you should leave now."

"Yes, sir," he said. Cary stood and held out his hand to shake. But Mr. Haynes just sat there and looked down at his desk, at some bills or invoices or whatever happened to be there. He didn't look at Cary. Cary set the frame upright on his desk and left.

On his way out of the store he nearly bumped into Dale, whose eyes were wide in concern. Cary tried to brush past him, but Dale pulled him aside, behind a toilet paper pyramid. "Here," he said, pulling at Cary's hand, placing in it a Valium. "One for the road."

Cary didn't even look at Dale, but he closed his fingers over the pill, moved away, and walked out the door into the parking lot. For an hour he sat there listening to the radio, hoping it would calm him. His hand remained closed, and when he finally opened it the pill had left tiny, white, sweaty streaks on his palm. He swallowed it dry. He felt it slide down his throat, heavy, like a lump, dissolving.

For the rest of the day, Cary drove around town, and for a few hours he sat in Monnish Park, which bordered his old high school. His classmates had always crossed the football fields to smoke here, but Cary never had. Today the park's benches and picnic pavilions were mostly empty; he figured the high schoolers had found other smoking spots, and this made him sad. When it got close to the time when schools let out, he drove to the Academy, Louise's school.

He arrived twenty minutes before the bell was supposed to ring, before Louise would walk out to her car, ready to raid Harco once again. He parked in a space that gave him a view of both the entrance to the school and her gaudy red Honda. He sat in his car, sweating, waiting for all of those carefree kids to get in their own cars and head home. He saw himself back then, all of those days when he rushed home as if that were the only place in the world he needed to be. Not worrying about the future, just knowing that things would somehow work out okay because they had to. Now he felt he had been cheated out of happiness. Things had not amounted to what they should have, people had not turned out the way he wanted them to. He didn't blame his father or his mother or anyone else for this—he figured that this disappointment was something that couldn't be altered one way or the other, that this was just the way things had to be. He tried not to think about what would happen next, but thoughts kept creeping in like cold drafts through cracks in a wall. He supposed he would go back to the university and finish, maybe even move back into his own apartment. Maybe call some of his friends. Study. Read books and learn. Go about the days with a purpose. Then find a job—no, a career. The bare outline of it seemed simple, but thinking about the actuality of it exhausted him. It all seemed like one big chore, as pointless as dusting.

But for now, at least, he had the Valium. It had started to make him feel good, light-headed and exuberant and bold. He heard the school bell ring, and there was a pause before the onslaught of high schoolers poured out the doors. He got out of his car and stood by the door, watching.

After the crowd of students had thinned, Cary saw Louise sauntering toward her car. She was wearing a black miniskirt and a loose, sleeveless white top, and her eyes were coated in bruiselike brown eye makeup. She carried no books, no purse, just her keys. He walked to her Honda and sat on its hood before she got there. She stopped when she saw him. She was only about ten feet away, looking at him with no expression.

"Hey, Louise."

She said nothing, just rattled her keys. There were others still around, but no one was paying them any attention.

"I was fired," he said. "But it's not your fault. I just wanted you to know that."

She crossed her arms over her chest but remained where she was.

"So you won't be seeing me anymore, at Harco, I mean." Cary smiled. He knew she wouldn't say anything, but he waited anyway, just to make her stand there, unable to get to her car.

When he returned to his car, Louise was sitting on her hood watching him. He drove past her slowly and honked the horn, and when he looked back in the rearview mirror, he was surprised to see her hold up her hand and offer a tiny, hesitant, but unmistakable wave.

I'm crying, I'm crying, I'm crying in my peas and carrots because the TV is broken again and I didn't lose weight on my Hollywood juice diet and Martin's sperm didn't take and I drank by myself this afternoon. Kahlúa and whole milk. I swore I wouldn't do that anymore.

"Next time," he says, swallowing his indifference as easily as his next forkful of food.

He is referring to the baby, of course, the one that won't come. I'm crying in my peas and carrots and getting fat on Kahlúa and he's telling me about next time. He pats my hand, which lies flat and cold on the formica tabletop. I know he means well, him with his gentle words. But it's hard to find solace in a man with white cream sauce in the corner of his mouth.

"You have white cream sauce in the corner of your mouth."

He wipes the wrong corner.

"Gone?" he asks.

"Yes," I say, and he turns his attention back to his food.

I watch him, this man I married after all those years of indecision. When he first asked me, straight out of high school, I'd said, not now. I expect to head out to Nevada to be a torch singer, I said, or to get commissioned by rich people to paint their portraits or see what it would feel like to be Mary Tyler Moore, working in a newsroom; to be the kind of girl who's going to make it after all. Marty waited for me;

he bided his time, understanding that none of these things would come to pass, and also that I would always wonder whether they would have if he didn't let me find out for myself. While I was getting nowhere, he worked his way up management at the Mazola plant, where he still works, coming home every day smelling like french fries.

When we dated he took me to places like the zoo and the cloisters, quiet places where, among other things, we talked about whether you can divide the world up into two kinds of people or not, and what those kinds might be and which we are.

On this late afternoon, this afternoon of Kahlúa and peas and carrots, I cry as if I might never stop because now I know that there *are* two kinds of people but I still don't know which kind I am. My husband sits with his back to the door leading to our yard, which opens up into a wild field thick with burnt-out waist-high grass. He eats so intently I wonder if he'll ever realize he's still got cream sauce on the corner of his mouth. I am wondering about the cream sauce on the corner of his mouth, and what kind of a boss Lou Grant would really make and just how many calories were in that Kahlúa, when the door slams open. My insides drop to the floor. I jump up and push my plate away. Martin swings around.

"What the hell?"

A slight man, dressed head to toe in black—from his Converse high-tops all the way up to his ski mask—stands before us. It is hard to tell what he is thinking because of the ski mask, but since he hesitates, I imagine he is confused, that he did not expect to find a husband with cream sauce on the corner of his mouth sitting across from a fat housewife crying into her peas and carrots.

"Your phone!" he shouts.

"Over there," I point at the phone.

"Damn it," he says. "It's attached to the wall."

"Yes," I say.

"It's a rotary," he says.

"I know."

"Everyone's gone cordless, cordless and touch-tone," he says.

"Not us."

"Nobody even makes these rotary wall phones anymore."

"I'm sorry," I say.

"Bitsy! What are you . . . what are you doing apologizing to this . . . this hoodlum?" Martin asks.

The hoodlum reaches into his jacket, pulls out a pistol, and waves it at Martin.

"Watch how you talk to the lady," the man in black says.

I fall back into my chair, in front of the peas and carrots. That chair feels like the only steady thing in this room, maybe even in the world.

"Hey, hey. Watch it now," Martin says, rising halfway from his seat. To himself, I'll bet he even sounds forceful and tough; he, my salvation, me, his damsel under duress.

"I don't think you are in a position to be making demands."

The man approaches Martin and holds the gun to his temple. Martin blanches. I imagine how cold that barrel must feel, how like a cannon instead of the small weapon it is.

"It's just that . . . just that . . . your weapon could discharge." Martin's face muscles twitch, and the twitching escalates into spasms, small ones at first, then bigger through his neck and his shoulders, until his whole body is racked with them. Finally, his legs collapse from under him, and Martin drops to the floor and crawls underneath the kitchen sink. I think this is my cue to go to him. Christ, I'll bet he's shit his pants even, but he should have known better and kept his mouth shut in the first place.

The intruder turns to me. "Who is this fool?"

"My husband, Martin."

"Tell Martin I know how to handle my weapon and then tell him he's got cream sauce on his mouth."

"All right," I say.

"You a good wife?" the masked man asks.

"I hope so."

"Because you should tell your husband about things like that; don't let him embarrass himself in front of strangers."

"We weren't expecting anyone."

"Didn't your mother always tell you to be ready to welcome unexpected guests into your home?"

"Not criminals," Martin whispers.

"You shut up," the masked man says, swerving the gun in Martin's direction again.

Martin shuts up.

The masked man picks up the phone and dials just three numbers.

"I'm the man you're looking for," he says into the receiver.

He pauses. "What do you mean which one? How many men you looking for who just robbed the only bank in this one-bank town?"

Another pause.

"Yes, I'll hold," he says. He turns to me, waves the gun at the fridge. "You got something to drink? A beer?"

"We have beer," I say.

I jump up too fast and get that dizzy feeling like the floor is rushing at me. The masked man grabs my elbow to steady me. The decency in the gesture, his touch, so unexpected, calms me, warms me.

"I'm all right," I say.

Hanging on to the table for support, I edge toward the refrigerator.

"Domestic or import?" I ask.

"Why, now we're talking. I'll take the import," he says.

But now I'm hanging on to the refrigerator door, not moving, my face immersed in the fluorescent glow, and I can't tell the milk from the cola from the devil's food cake from the ham sandwich from yesterday's meatloaf, and for the life of me I can't make out which of these abstract shapes is a beer bottle, import or not, but I won't cry, I won't cry.

"Why is she crying?" the masked man asks my husband.

I look at Martin. He seems shrunken; his head is bowed, half-hidden by a drain pipe. He shrugs his shoulders.

"Don't you care why your own wife's crying?"

But Martin doesn't get a chance to answer because someone is on the line now talking to our visitor. I watch his hand grip the receiver tighter, the veins and tendons swelling with his speech, strong, terse.

"Hello, Officer. There is an armed intruder holding two people hostage at 555 Dale Drive. I believe he might be dangerous. . . . Yes, I am that very gentleman." He smiles mischievously at me, like he and I are in on this together. It's impossible not to return the smile. I remember Martin and turn to him. He has the look of a man who just caught his wife doing unspeakable things with another man.

As the stranger continues to talk I snap to, find the beer, the bottle opener in the silverware drawer, pop the bottle open, drop the cap in the recycling bin, and hand it to him.

"What a nice lady," he says, slugging from the bottle. The beer's half gone by the time he pulls it away from his lips. "Would be a damn shame if something bad happened to her."

As he continues to talk the sound of sirens approaches. I peek out the front window curtain. Police cars are grinding to a halt on our lawn, willy-nilly across the azalea beds and freshly mown grass, and officers in hard vests are pouring out, their guns trained on us. The police lights cast a swirling, ceaseless glow across the kitchen walls. Static hisses from walkie-talkies, inaudible, jumbled voices crying commands, dispatched from some safe place where they don't want to mess up from because a thing like this doesn't happen every day, because a thing like this, if it goes wrong, could cost them their jobs.

Our neighbors pour out of their houses and congregate on the blocked-off street, whispering—Mrs. Annie Ardley, whose divorce papers came through yesterday, whispering to the Gradys, who just had their twins, whispering to little Thomas, fourteen now, who broke his sister's arm last week when she aggravated him over a misplaced shirt. There are more, many more, crawling out of their homes like aliens from pods, glad they're not us, but glad to be here to see it. It could get grisly.

A more official-looking man than the other officers (he wears a suit, not a uniform, and no hard vest) emerges from a car with his loudspeaker in hand. It's clear he's their leader because he's got the look of a guy who doesn't get surprised by anything anymore. I let the curtain drop back into place.

"Mr. Urchin," he says at the house. "Wick Urchin."

"Is that your name?" I ask. "Wick Urchin?"

"No," he says. "But you can call me Urchin. That's what people sometimes call me."

"Okay, Urchin."

"It's not so bad yet, Mr. Urchin," the man outside says. "All you did was attempt—I *stress,* attempt—to rob First Nationwide. It's a felony. I won't lie to you, but I can see here on your record, you're pretty clean. You can walk away from this."

"Don't believe him," Urchin says to me. "I've got a rap sheet longer . . . I was gonna say longer than your husband's spine, but I can see . . ." He doesn't need to say the rest. He laughs.

I whirl around. Martin's face is now completely obscured, buried in his arms, which are wrapped around his knees. He rocks back and forth like he just got sprung from Sweet Meadows Asylum a month too soon.

"Is Bitsy really what they call you?"

"Don't you like it?" I ask.

"Sure," he says. "But your mother didn't really name you Bitsy, did she? It's not your real name, is it?"

"My real name is Elizabeth," I tell Urchin.

"Elizabeth," he says, and I can see his eyes crinkling in a smile. "Like the queen."

And as he says it, I suddenly feel regal, and beautiful, the way I felt when I drank my Kahlúa today and put on the Johnny Mathis record and my black lace bustier, the one with the imitation pearl décolletage, and ran my hands over my breasts as I watched myself, luxurious and spilling over, in the standing mirror. For a moment I'd thought maybe I'd fallen in love with myself. I was beautiful, but there hadn't been anyone there to see it.

"Like the queen," I say, falling in love with myself all over again, this time with someone here to see it.

The phone rings. Urchin picks it up.

"It's for you," he says, holding it out to Martin. But Martin simply shakes his head, unable to speak. I take the receiver.

"We're fine," I say in response to the policeman on the other end of the line. "But he's got a gun."

"I'm not frightened," I say, and again Urchin smiles. Somehow his approval fills me. I remember a line I read in the Bible, I think, a line so beautiful and poetic and unfathomable until now:

I am replete with the very thee.

I want him to feel as I do. He fills me.

I return the phone to Urchin and wander into the pantry, with its narrow glassed-in shelves. My hand, I notice, is only trembling slightly now as I open the delicately frosted cabinet door, with its wisteria etching framing it. I am going to cook. A huge pot of soup. I've got chicken stock, and bouillon cubes for flavor, and cornstarch, and flour and potatoes to thicken the broth, and in the fridge there are nearly fresh vegetables from the green market: celery stalks—I'll still have to trim the leaves—and carrots, which need peeling, and scallions and sweet Vidalia onions, and clove upon clove of garlic which need mincing. I'll make us a pot of soup, and fill the house with the smell of it, and watch it simmer with Urchin when he is not taking calls. When it's finished I'll pour a big bowl of it for him, and he can have as much as he wants. And I will sit across from him as he eats my soup.

"What did I tell you?" Urchin booms from the kitchen, his voice escalating.

"It's true. I was born at night. But not last night, you incompetent—"

I hurry back toward the kitchen, my arms full with the bag of flour and bouillon cubes and garlic vines and chicken stock, but before I get there, there is a crack, like the world coming to an end, and the shattering of glass from the back window, and a thud—a thud so heavy and definite even I know what it is. And I see the sniper who'd been lying in wait like a snake in the field out back, maybe waiting for me to get out of his sight line—slithering out of the weeds, as a jumble of blue men flood my kitchen, their guns waving wildly in case they still have a target to shoot at. And then I see him, Urchin, on the floor, bleeding from his neck, his eyes still open, but no longer smiling.

I drop the food and the flour poofs across the front of my dress as it hits the floor. Urchin is still wearing his mask, but I don't wait to see what he looks like when they take it off.

An officer has thrown a blanket over Martin's shoulders. He is shaking, but not because he is cold. He opens his mouth as if he has something important to tell me. His words are nearly inaudible.

"Next time," Martin says again, only now he means it.

But I barely hear him. All I hear is what resonates in my head: the crack of a gun, the thud of Urchin's body as it falls to the floor, the shattering of glass, the crush of policemen pushing through the door and scattering through this house, no longer my own, a legion of strangers splitting and dividing like cancerous cells. I don't know them, but I know what the crack of a gun sounds like, and I know how it sounds when a man gets killed. This is what they have given me.

I step over the spilled groceries and exit through the door Urchin came in from. I head out to the field, away from the commotion, the camera crews, and flashing lights, and neighbors, away from Martin, who is probably too shaken up to notice that I've gone. I walk and I walk away from the smell of gunpowder and white cream sauce, and the wind rises up and blows the flour off my dress like sand across dunes, and as I continue to walk west, wading through the knee-high weeds, I notice that my abdomen is swelling, too subtle at first to be certain, and too obvious then not to be, and I notice, placing my hand on the firm, warm swell, that I just happen to be walking in the direction of the setting sun.

BLACK COWBOY

Carmen Elena Mitchell

At my door is Jesse, all grown up. Six feet tall, with dark curls, wearing presents on his head.

The 1930s leather cowboy hat and lasso are from the character he's playing in Hollywood's latest version of American History: Black cowboy saves town, teaches White girl to love. The miniature wooden pipe on a leather string around his neck is from his costar. The diamond stud in his ear is from a forty-year-old married lady.

His dark skin glows like there's a light underneath it. He smells like the road.

When we were young he was a spidery, long-legged boy with too much hair. We would wrestle in piles with the other kids after school. Later in high school he was a tall, looming Othello, to my quivering Desdemona. In college, he did a dog food commercial and learned to drink beer from the bottom of the can. He showed me how when he'd come back on holidays, while I wiped cinnamon roll onto my apron at the diner. Saving up for someday, I'd tell him.

But we were friends once upon a time.

And now here he is looking so tall and rich under the lonely, swinging bulb that is my trailer home. And here I am in "someday," three states later. Different diner.

In the film he saves a white girl from drowning. The mayor's daughter. He starts out as a bandit. But then he saves her. She saves him from banditry. Their love saves the town from ruin. One of them is going to have to die in the end, but the producers haven't figured out which. They are shooting on location in a city just north of here.

Jesse will stay with me in this small Midwestern town for a week before he goes back to complete the shoot. He will stay with me and feed my plants and make me leave the trailer occasionally to go dancing. He will make me love the hills again. He will make my friends seem interesting. I will make him chili.

Tonight I make him chili. He thinks we should add beer to it. But, no, we must follow the recipe. I am adamant. This is the only thing I know how to make that doesn't come in a box. That involves measuring spoons. It is the secret of a small town in the Midwest famous for its chili. A leaked recipe. Top with grated cheese and scallions. Serve over spaghetti. It is perfume. We have his beer as a side and eat on our laps.

Tonight after dinner we drive to a gay bar. A small, dark window in a quiet alley that flashes BAR in red neon. Sunflowers growing up in the garbage outside. Enter through the secret door. Inside it is all palm trees and plastic fruit. Men in dresses, men in chaps, big men in baseball caps, imprints of wedding rings on their sunburned fingers. Several women in flannel with long, tiered hair and plain faces. The only nightlife I find bearable in this small, Midwestern town. I was a regular here once upon a time. A skinny black-eyed susan among the sunflowers, and slugs. They know me here. They kiss me here.

Jesse and I lean into each other at the bar. I look up at the angles of his cheekbones, his full lips that looked so odd on him when he was younger. His face has grown into something made for the long, slow glances of film.

The boys love him. They tell me, "Good goin', girlfriend. Are you sure he's straight?"

He is watching them like a foreign film. He asks me to translate handkerchiefs, and mustaches. What do they mean? I ask him if it reminds him of the frat house. All that aftershave and muscle. The dance of men's bodies.

Jesse buys me shots of Jaegermeister. I'm thinking he's trying to get me drunk. All week we've been drinking and getting stoned and sitting together on the futon.

Tonight we stumble home, almost too loaded to talk. We sit on the futon, heads bobbing, and he tells me about a party on the set. How he and his costar, a good-looking, blond cowboy who is all teeth (the one the white girl's supposed to marry), and some other man, some big-talking, graying Hollywood type, stayed late on into the night. Doing shots. How Jesse collapsed next to the punch bowl, fishing for pineapple. How someone slumped on a sofa, watching through a bottle of champagne, unable to move, told him later how Hollywood had pushed Jesse's limp body up against the back of a couch. How he'd undone Jesse's belt and slid his pants down to his knees. Through the bottle, watching the whole time, the fat pink and mahogany of their skins collide. Big pink flaps crashing in waves.

"It's fucked up," he says, staring out into the cold in front of him. We are floating in a fog, his form appearing and disappearing. Waving at each other from two pieces of a sinking ship. Hold on tight to the brown bottle. Peel the label. Take a another drink from a broken oar.

"No one else knows."

I'm sorry.

Jesse was the first boy I ever kissed. Seventh grade, truth or dare. Boy-girl party in someone's pink bedroom under the lacy canopy. It took me forever. I was terrified of missing his lips. His big, dark eyes, rimmed in their curly, boy lashes, so patient while I calculated angles.

Tonight too goes on and on. He touches my leg, slaps a hand on my thigh. A signal. It's been over a decade since seventh grade. I turn to kiss him. The room rotates, and is swallowed by the black of my dress going over my head. We are at strange angles. We roll over and over banging into chairs and upturning the wobbly, splintering spool that serves as a coffee table.

Now my back is kissing cold linoleum. Now I am biting his ear. Now he is scraping my skin off with his fingernails. Now there is blood and he is whispering drunkenly into my neck.

"You know, you have your period."

I sit up, loosening myself from him. There is blood coating my legs, in sticky, body prints across the linoleum, on him. The horror of red disappearing into brown. I run from the trail. Under the blinking fluorescent light in the tiny bathroom I look down. There is so much. It keeps coming. It is too red, too bright, too flat. It is all wrong. Months of missed periods converging. I stand in the shower, leaning back against the wall and let the cold hit me. Hard little nails pinning me to the plastic wall. I sit on the toilet, dripping and shivering, my head curled over on my lap. Holding down the nausea. Trembling, whispering curses to myself.

I find a towel and creep back into the room. A pad and some sweats in the shallow closet. He has pulled out the futon, and is lying facedown in the middle, his clothes back on. There is an icy space next to him. I sit in the middle of it. In the other corner is the cushioned window seat, like the side of a ship. Pull up the lid to find my snowy down comforter. Remnants of home, and a big princess bed. From the days when I reigned. Before the crown fell. A big pillow to bury myself under.

I sleep in the window, against the cold glass—cocooned in feathers, feeling the pad between my legs.

The next day he is not there when I get home from work. He has washed the floor. My dress is hanging on the laundry line outside. My plants repositioned as to better catch the sun.

He comes back later with no words. We fall asleep together on the futon. Under the glaze of TV, movie star lovemaking flashes across our noses.

The next morning he leaves in a cab. His cowboy hat back on. His lasso circling his shoulder. His pipe forgotten on the coffee table. Tired but ready for more adventures. A quick kiss, on the side of the mouth, not looking into my eyes.

I am waiting here to meet a man I've never met, to do things I've never done before with another man. I don't know what he looks like, or how old he is, or even his name. All I have is a promise to meet here in the Pinball Palace, today, at six o'clock. And already he is twenty minutes late.

I'm going to wait a little longer, just to see if he shows up. Because you have to wonder what kind of guy would actually do this. I move through the crowds, trying to spot him before he spots me. Some people I can rule out immediately: guys in groups, guys with women, guys pushing baby strollers. But after that, it's hard. The arcade is full of high school boys and frat boys and paperboys. A tattooed skater punk is kicking the Lethal Enforcers game. An off-duty security guard drops quarters into a pinball machine. I move around them all, not staying in any one place too long. This guy—the one I'm looking for—he could be *anyone*.

1.

My name is Richard Szatowski and I am twenty years old. I lost my virginity at age thirteen, and since then I've had more girlfriends than any guy working in this mall. There's always someone new, and she's always very beautiful and very feminine: long hair, slender legs, full breasts. I've been asked to six proms, three college formals, a zillion weddings, and already one class reunion. I've slept with the Assistant

Manager of CD World, with the head of the Macy's gift wrap department, and with nearly all the girls working at Old Navy. I've been in the same relationship for the last four months; we have sex several times a week and my girlfriend claims it is the best she's ever had. Now, I'm not saying any of this to brag—I just want you to know where I stand.

The trouble started three days ago, Tuesday morning, as Shereen and I were on the verge of another fight.

"Basic?" She sat up in bed, leaning on her elbow. "What do you mean, basic?"

I put my arm around her. "Not in a bad way—"

"You *said,* 'It just gets basic after a while.'"

"It does."

"It does?"

"Why are you taking this the wrong way?"

She pulled back, lifting the blankets up to her shoulders. "You're saying you're bored."

"I didn't say *that.*" I moved my hand across her waist, pinching her hip, and she slapped at it like she'd been stung.

"Don't," she warned.

So I rolled onto my stomach, my face shoved into a pillow. "Whatever."

I was *not* bored. Shereen had a great body and she knew it, so I'm not sure why she was giving me attitude. I was just trying to explain what I saw as a simple fact of life: once you got used to a person, no matter who they were, sex would become familiar, monotonous. In other words, *basic.*

Shereen would take something like that the wrong way. Even after four months, she still didn't trust me. She still monitored the friends I went out with, making sure there were never any girls, and I always had to lie if I went to a nudie bar. She wouldn't believe that I only went to drink and hang out, that the dancers on stage did very little for me. She was convinced I would leave her for the next beautiful woman I met.

A little later Shereen got up and went into the bathroom, my blankets draped around her shoulders and waist. Before turning on the shower she made a big show of locking the door. I just sprawled out on my bed, enjoying the extra space. It was a twin, not wide enough for two people, and when she stayed over I never slept well.

We set off for the mall in silence. I drove, and Shereen sat in the passenger seat, holding her overnight bag in her lap. "You're not staying tonight?" I asked, just to be sure.

She shook her head. "And it doesn't get *basic* after a while. If anything, it gets more meaningful—more complex—which just shows how little you know what you're talking about."

I shrugged. "All right."

"Don't all right me." She crossed her arms over her chest. "You're bored, is what it is. I'm boring you."

"No, you're not."

"Is there something you want to try?" she asked. "Some kind of—"

"No."

"You don't even want to try?"

"I *do*. Just forget what I said."

One night a few weeks ago, I was hanging about the mall food court, waiting for the 6:30 bus. A nearby pay phone was ringing and ringing, some fifteen or twenty times. Finally I walked over and answered.

"Yes," a man said, "my name is Lawrence Donovan and I'm calling on behalf of the Ross Marketing agency. Would you care to take part in a consumer fashion survey?"

I was just killing time, anyway. "Sure."

He took my name, my age, my permanent address, my telephone number, my height (5'8") and my weight (160). He explained that the survey was about women's fashion and asked if I was currently involved with someone. I told him I was, and answered his questions about Shereen. She was my age, my height, slim, with kinky brown hair that fell to her shoulders and wide brown eyes. "And what kind of outfits do you prefer her in?" he asked. I told him just about anything; Shereen is a stylist for Glamour Shots, so looking good comes natural to her. "You're lucky," he joked.

"I know."

Still laughing, he asked if she wore any lingerie that was out of the ordinary. I thought he was kidding, then realized he wasn't.

"I guess not," I said. "Pretty much normal stuff."

"Normal, as in . . ."

"I don't know. Bras? Underwear?"

"Would you enjoy seeing her in something more risqué?"

"I don't know. I never thought about it."

"Think about it now," he told me. "Imagine Shereen in a black silk camisole and matching thong bikini, wearing nothing else. On your bed. Describe her to me."

And by then I guess I knew that it wasn't a fashion survey, that this Lawrence Donovan was some kind of nut. But I didn't hang up.

"I don't know," I said.

"Don't know what?" he asked. "Come on. Visualize."

"I can't."

"You can."

"No," I told him. "There's someone on the phone next to me."

He paused. "I understand," he said. "But you've fucked her?"

"Yes."

"Up the ass?"

"No. That's disgusting."

"What about blow jobs?"

"Yes."

"Good?"

"Yes."

"You go down on her?"

"No," I said. "She thinks that's disgusting, too."

"Do you?"

"I don't care either way."

"Have you tried phone sex?"

"No."

"I could call you at home," he said.

And I realized just how much I'd told this man: He knew my phone number, my address, my girlfriend's address. He knew what we looked like. "I'll call the police," I said. "I swear to God."

"Don't be a cunt," he hissed.

I hung up. In another ten minutes I was on the bus, feeling sick to my stomach, and then I got off and walked the rest of the way to my apartment. When I arrived home, the red light on my answering machine was blinking; it was another hour before I built up the nerve to play my messages, and when I finally did they were only from my mother.

But then my phone starting ringing in the middle of the night—12:30, 1:30, four in the morning. I never answered and it was never a problem unless Shereen stayed over. "Why don't you get that?" she'd ask, half-asleep.

"Too tired," I'd answer in a groggy voice, even though the sound of the telephone had jarred me awake. I'd switch off the ringer and then try to fall back asleep. Shereen suspected another woman, of course, but after two weeks the calls just stopped, and that was the end of that.

But in a weird way, I wasn't as relieved as I thought I'd be. Because I still found myself wondering: What kind of guy would actually do that?

I sell sneakers at the Foot Locker for six bucks an hour—no commission, no benefits. That Tuesday morning, by the time I finished arguing with Shereen and stopped off for a Pepsi, I was twenty minutes late. My boss is a stickler for punctuality. He's tall, well-built, and wears the same clothes as his employees: black and white referee jerseys, black sweats, white sneakers. He was searching for a foot measurer when I arrived, then grabbed the whistle hanging from his neck and blew into it. "Number forty-four!" he shouted. "You're late!"

I walked over. "Sorry, Coach."

"Late again, I'll slap you with a penalty."

Coach always talked like that. In the mornings, before the store opened, he'd pull us into a big huddle and outline sales strategies.

"You're doing inventory this morning," he said, and placed a thick black marker into my hand. "Start with the Reeboks." Then he pushed me away and slapped my behind; I sprung forward and splashed Pepsi all over my referee jersey.

"Easy, sport," he laughed. "Something the matter?"

"No, no, everything's fine," I told him.

Coach is what you'd call a touchy-feely person. The word in the mall is that he used to teach high school athletics in Delaware; an incident occurred involving two of the Junior Varsity boys, and the Board of Education fired him. I don't know how anyone could have found this out, so maybe it's bullshit—but I wouldn't put it past him, either.

I grabbed a clean referee jersey and then walked to the nearest men's rest room, which was directly across from the food court. It was empty when I arrived, but I changed in a stall, anyway. I tried to remind myself that Coach was just a very physical person. And no one else seemed to mind the way he acted—the other guys were always clapping him on the back, or bumping butts when someone scored a good sale. Like it was all normal behavior.

After changing shirts, I lowered the toilet seat and sat down, not wanting to return to work just yet. Once I was sick with a stomach virus and sat in the very same stall for twenty minutes, reading graffiti and playing with squares of toilet paper. A man had entered the stall next to mine, dropped his pants, and began to masturbate. Right there on the toilet. He didn't even try to hide it. His shoes slid back and forth across the tiled floor, sometimes extending all the way under the divider, into my stall. I had wanted to get up but couldn't—not because I was sick, that was gone—but because for some reason I felt obligated to stay. As if we were sharing the experience.

Today I was alone. The walls surrounding me were covered in graffiti: crude drawings of women getting fucked by gigantic cocks, their legs spread at 180-degree angles; lots of names and numbers—women with big tits, men with big dicks, girls with deep throats. And everything started with the words "I want." *I WANT TO GET FUCKED. I WANT A BABY-SITTER WITH A TIGHT PUSSY AND FLAT CHEST. I WANT TO SUCK THROBBING YOUNG COCK.* I want, I want, I want. It made *me* almost want to beat off, right there in the stall, but I wasn't bold enough to risk it. I had friends who worked for mall security, and they were always patrolling for wackos.

But looking back, I wish maybe I had, because perhaps then I wouldn't have made the mistake I did. After listening to make sure there was still no one else in the room, I took the black inventory marker out of my pocket and, underneath the words *I WANT TO SUCK THROBBING YOUNG COCK,* I hastily scribbled back *ME TOO.*

That same night I made up with Shereen. She came over at eight and I cooked us both dinner: spaghetti, red wine, and Häagen-Dazs. I apologized a hundred times, insisting I loved her over and over until I convinced both of us it was true. Then together we proved it, making love in my bathtub, the showerhead raining down on us.

Afterward we lay in bed, spent, the sheets damp from our bodies. I felt exhausted but at least the guilt was gone; I'd tried erasing the words, scrubbing them off the wall with wet toilet paper, but the marker was permanent and now they were there for all the world to see. *ME TOO.* I regretted writing them immediately, but of course it was too late. I shoved the soda-stained shirt in my knapsack and fled.

Shereen rolled on top of me, stroking my chin with her fingertip. "And how was that?"

"Awesome," I said. She rested her face on my chest and closed her eyes.

It was a long time before she spoke again. "My parents are having their anniversary dinner on Friday. They want you to come."

"And meet your *family?*"

She sat up. "Yes. And Meet Them."

"I'm kidding. I'll go."

Shereen reached under the sheets and pinched my thigh. "You better go, you—"

I flipped her off me, rolled on top, and pinned her shoulders to the bed. She beat her fists against my chest, threw back her head, and shrieked. Everything, I decided, was going to be all right.

And everything was fine for the next three days—Wednesday, Thursday, Friday. Shereen stayed over every night and we made love constantly, all over the apartment, the way we did when we first started dating. There were no mystery phone calls in the middle of the night; even my boss had backed off, too busy with business to goose his employees. That Friday afternoon, just before I had to meet Shereen, I stopped in the rest room to wash up.

I hadn't been there since Tuesday. Someone was using the stall I'd changed in; as I entered, he stood up and flushed the toilet. I leaned over the sink, washing my hands and face, watching for him in the mirror. Finally the door opened and he came out: a huge black guy in a Gold's Gym T-shirt, with a barrel chest and enormous biceps. I looked down to the sink, inspecting my palms. He grabbed some paper towels and left.

I dried my hands on my jeans and walked out, through the mall, as far as the Hallmark store before turning around and walking all the way back. I closed the door to the stall and locked it. Underneath the words *I WANT TO SUCK THROBBING YOUNG COCK* and underneath the words *ME TOO,* someone had written:

2/24—6:00—Arcade. Green Cap.

I didn't even have to look at my watch. I knew that the day was today, and the time was only an hour away, and that my life had suddenly become a lot more complicated.

2.

He is now more than twenty minutes late.

Or is he? Maybe he's the Korean man sitting on the bench next to me, a cluster of shopping bags around his feet. Or the guy in the biker jacket who just walked out of the arcade, the one in the Harley shirt with the frizzy hair. How should I know? I haven't seen anyone wearing a green cap. I realize maybe that's not what the message meant— maybe *I'm* supposed to be wearing the green cap, so he can spot *me*. But I won't let that happen. Right now, I want to be invisible.

Shereen had been furious, of course. I went by Glamour Shots to tell her I couldn't make dinner, that something had come up. And she started shouting over the ear-splitting dance music that I had no right to do this to her.

"I'm sorry," I'd said. "I forgot about this thing my parents are having. For *their* anniversary."

"*Their* anniversary? Today?"

"Yeah—"

"They have the same anniversary as *my* parents, and you *forgot?*"

"You know I'm terrible with dates—"

"You're not a very good liar, either." Two of the photographers overheard this and tittered. "I can always tell when you're lying."

"I'm not lying."

"Then just come by for an hour," she said. "Can you do that? Can you spare an hour?"

The funny thing is, part of me really wanted to go. Part of me couldn't resist a big family dinner, with grandparents and godparents and lots of little kids running around, with hot covered dishes and homemade desserts and everyone teasing me and Shereen, the two lovebirds, about when we were getting married.

"Maybe," I said. "I can't promise anything—"

"Then forget it," Shereen said, and away she went, through a door marked EMPLOYEES ONLY, even as I called her name. The photographers looked down at their platform shoes and burst into giggles.

But no matter: I'll be at Shereen's in less than an hour, ready to apologize again, with fresh flowers or a box of Godiva chocolates. I only want to stay here a little longer, to see what this guy looks like. If he shows up. Because you *really* have to wonder what kind of guy would do this.

Someone taps me on the shoulder. "Do you have the time?"

I look up. Facing me is a man in his early fifties, short and heavyset, in a white shirt and light blue tie. His face is pink and fleshy, his forehead creased with wrinkles. He reminds me of a pharmacist.

"No," I say.

He pinches the brim of his Oakland A's hat, pulling it down over his forehead. "I was supposed to meet someone, but I'm running late."

"Sorry," I tell him. "My girlfriend's running late, too."

He apologizes for disturbing me and walks into the arcade. So maybe he's not a pharmacist, I think—maybe he's a businessman. The clothes and wristwatch suggest that he's well off. But this man lacks a businessman's confidence; he slinks around the arcade, like he's getting ready to shoplift something. He studies the guys on Mortal Kombat for five seconds, then moves on. His methods are obvious:

Ignore the ones in groups, the ones with girlfriends, the ones with children. The whole time I'm watching, he doesn't even approach another
person. Finally he leaves the Pinball Palace and walks away, disappearing into the crowds.

I catch up to him in front of Banana Republic. "Hey," I say. "Are
you—"

He recognizes me and nods. "Green cap."

"Yeah."

"I thought you were the one," he says. He extends his hand and I
notice crescents of sweat under his arms. "Dennis," he says. "Dr.
Dennis Mulvey."

I wipe my palms on my jeans and shake. "Brad."

"Just Brad?"

"Just Brad," I say. His grip is strong, a doctor's handshake. He isn't
lying about his profession.

Then we're both standing silent again. "I guess I ought to be honest with you," Dennis finally admits. "I've never done this before."

"Done what?"

"Met someone. This way. To do what we're going to do."

"What are we going to do?" I ask.

His face flushes. "I guess that's up to you," he says. "There's a bar
off Route 18—"

"I want to stay in the mall."

"Okay," he says.

"Is that all right?"

"Sure."

"I'd like to get some Chinese food," I decide.

"All right," he says.

So we walk toward the Golden Wok Restaurant. I'm moving fast,
trying not to look at him, but at the same time I want to learn everything I can. I smell the Old Spice he's wearing, the same cologne my
father's used for the last twenty years. I listen to the inseams of his

pants sweeping together, faded and worn by his short stumpy legs. And I can hear his labored breathing as he struggles to keep up with my nervous strides.

"You must be hungry," he calls.

I slow down a little. "I don't want to see anyone I know. I work here."

"So do I."

"You said you were a doctor."

"In Lenscrafters," he says. "I'm an optometrist."

"Oh."

"Where do you work?" he asks.

"Circuit City," I tell him. "And look, would you mind not staring at me?"

He only moves closer. "What?"

"The way you're looking at me. People can tell."

Dennis frowns. "I'm sorry," he says, but he keeps right on looking anyway. I wonder what he sees. My body is in much better shape than his. I'm lean and muscular from working out; women have told me I have a nice smile and a great ass. Would a man notice these things? Would Dr. Mulvey? And what does he have to offer me in return? He's fat, he's old, he's losing his hair. He must realize I have the advantage.

We are seated in a far corner of Golden Wok at a small table for two; a single candle burns between us. An anonymous waiter comes for our order.

"Wonton soup," I say.

"This is on me," Dennis says. "Order what you want."

I close my menu and hand it to the waiter. "Just soup."

Dennis orders something called the Phoenix and Dragon, then folds his hands and studies me from across the table.

"So," he says.

"What?"

He shrugs. "Nothing."

I stick my finger in the candle, prodding the melted wax. A warm layer of it coats my fingertip. Then I accidentally push too hard and snuff out the flame.

"I've got matches," Dennis says, reaching into his pants pocket. He comes up with a heaping handful of spare change, at least four dollars' worth, and picks through it, plucking out half a pack of Breath Savers, a Visine dropper bottle and, finally, a small Bic lighter.

I spot a gold wedding band amidst the silver and copper coins. "You're married?"

"Yes."

"Why aren't you wearing the ring?"

Dennis shrugs and puts it back on his finger. Then he removes his hands from the table. I relight the candle.

"Does she know?" I ask.

He shakes his head. "She suspects."

"Which is worse?"

"Does your girlfriend know?"

"How did you know I had a girlfriend?"

"You said you did," he tells me. "You said you were waiting for her."

"That was a lie," I say.

"Oh."

"If I had a girlfriend, why would I be here with you?"

"I don't know."

"Think about it," I say. "Does that make any sense?"

"I guess not. You're young. You can do what you want."

"Oh, you think so?"

"When you get to be my age," he says, "and you realize certain things? And you've got a family? It's too late. Unless you want to lose everything."

I don't say anything. Dennis reaches across the table and pours us both some tea. "You've been in a lot of relationships," he says.

"Yeah."

"I meant, with other men."

"I know what you meant. Yes, I have."

Dennis sips his tea and I can tell he's disappointed. It takes him a while to find the right words. "When I said I'd never done this before," he begins, "I meant everything. I mean, never. Nothing."

I try to look disappointed. "It's no big deal."

"You're sure?"

"It isn't to me if it isn't to you," I say, and I smile, and Dennis leans back in his chair, relieved.

"I'm so glad I just told you that," he confesses. "I'm so glad all the cards are on the table now."

Our food comes. I finish my soup fast but Dennis takes a long time with his meal. He keeps offering me some and I keep refusing until, finally, I wave the waiter over and ask for an extra plate.

He tells me about himself. Dennis graduated pre med from Penn State in 1970 and received his optometry degree six years later. He met his wife in '78; she came into his office with a tear duct problem and they were married within the year. His wallet is full of photographs: Dennis and Mrs. Mulvey, holding hands in front of a Christmas tree; Dennis and his ten-year-old son, waiting in line at Space Mountain; Dennis and his teenage daughter, seated side-by-side on a piano bench. He's your basic family man: homework helper, Little League director, conscientious member of the PTA.

I tell him my last relationship was with a man who used to coach high school basketball in Delaware. "A real big guy, built like an ox," I say. "But a total control freak."

Dennis shifts in his chair, uneasy, just as the waiter appears with our check. The doctor pays the bill and we're ready to leave. "I'm parked out by the movie theater," he says. "We can go in my van."

"Where will we go?"

He pauses. "I thought we'd just go in my van."

"Oh."

"I can't stay away from home all night."

"No. Neither can I."

"You're sure?"

"The van's fine," I say.

"Now?"

"I don't care."

So we pick up and leave. Back in the mall, business is winding down; the stores will be open for just another hour. As we pass the display windows, Dennis asks if there's anything I need, if I have enough money, if there's anything I'd like him to buy.

"No."

"Anything," he says.

We exit the mall under the bright lights of the Loews theater marquee. It's freezing outside and groups of moviegoers are huddled together in line, hands shoved in pockets, scarves wrapped over faces. I recognize a bunch of them: friends from Waldenbooks and Eddie Bauer and F.A.O. Schwartz. They wave to us and I smile back, praying to God I won't have to introduce Dennis. We both must look so obvious. We may as well be holding hands.

Dennis stops and points. "Do you know those people?" he asks.

"Just keep walking," I whisper, and steer him toward the parking lot.

We walk all the way out to Q12, the most distant corner of the parking lot, which most people only use during the Christmas shopping season. Dennis turns on the engine and starts up the heat, but after ten minutes the van is still freezing. There are no windows in the back but no seats, either, just a cold corrugated metal floor. The ceiling is too low for either of us to stand, so for a while we just pace around, hunched over, and wait for the van to warm up. Then Dennis uncovers some lawn chairs from a long-ago family beach trip; he unfolds two and we sit down across from each other.

Another ten minutes pass, probably more. I can hear Dennis breathing fast, can see the condensation of his breath and the faint outline of his face. I'm supposed to be the one with the experience, so I slide my hand up his thigh; Dennis exhales, leaning back in his chair. I can feel him through his pants, smaller than I expected but already hard and wedged up against his thigh. I kneel before him, help him unbutton his trousers, and slide them to his knees. "Oh, God," he sighs.

"Don't talk."

I fumble for his dick through the flap of his boxer shorts.

"Oh, God," Dennis murmurs. "Oh, God. Oh, God."

"Shut up," I whisper, and take him in my mouth.

Dennis comes fast but I take longer. I make him remove all his clothes and then all of mine, provoking him with small insults until he's yanking and tearing them off my body. "You're so strong," I say, mocking him, and he grabs at my white briefs, ripping them down the seam. "Tear them off," I say. He does. I scissor my legs around his neck and grip the back of his head, pulling at his hair, pressing his face between my thighs. "Come on," I say. "Come on." I slouch down, forcing my cock deeper into his mouth. "Come on." His head bobs faster in response to my command. I close my eyes and hear the voice of Lawrence Donovan, ordering me to visualize; I feel the slap of Coach's hand on my ass; I see the black muscleman in the Gold's Gym shirt, sitting in a bathroom stall, throbbing young cock in hand. Dennis spreads his fingers over my thighs, tickling my skin and teasing my balls. Then I explode into his mouth and he takes all of it, everything, not stopping even when I'm pushing him away, when I'm kicking him away. "Stop it," I say. *"Stop."*

He pulls back, grinning, and swallows. "What?"

My legs drop off his shoulders. "Just stop," I say, shuddering. "That's enough."

I sit back. Dennis rests his head on my knees, kissing my thighs, and massages my feet with his hands. I catch my breath. It has never been like this before. I have never exploded into a woman's mouth, not like that. I'm never left gasping for air.

But the minutes pass and I compose myself. It is hot and I ask Dennis to turn off the heat. He stands up and steps awkwardly across the van, the excess flesh hanging from his body in folds. He is an unattractive man. And look at me—talking like a faggot already. I read once that just because a person had one homosexual experience, that didn't mean they were a homosexual. Why did I just waste my one shot with a slob like Dennis Mulvey?

He kneels down and places his head in my lap. I put my palm on his forehead and push him away.

"What's wrong?" he asks.

"You mean what's wrong with *you*," I say. I stand up and shake out my clothes.

"What's that supposed to mean?"

"It means what it means," I say, standing up. "There's nothing wrong with *me*."

He's confused. "What are you doing?"

"We're done, aren't we?"

"I don't know," he says.

"We're done."

"I did something wrong," he sighs, and I don't let him think that he didn't. I shake out my jeans and step into them, not even bothering to look for my underwear.

Dennis drags the lawn chair in front of his body, suddenly self-conscious. "Brad," he asks. "Did I do something wrong?"

"Do you think you did?"

"I don't know."

I pull on my shirt. "That's the thing. You don't even know. You have no concept of it."

"No concept of what?"

"If I were just two years younger," I say, "you could be arrested."

I reach for my sneakers and uncover the tattered remains of my white briefs; I shove them in my back pocket and then lace up my Nikes. Dennis holds his head in his hands. It serves him right, I think. He should be crying.

I open the door to the van. "You can't just leave," he says. "I thought—"

"You thought what?"

He holds out his hands. "I thought we'd stay friends."

"That's not what this was."

"But Brad—"

I shake my head. "My name's not Brad."

A blast of frigid air blows into the van and Dennis cowers behind the lawn chair, holding it over his body like an awkward blanket. I jump out and sprint across the parking lot; for a while I can't find my car and I panic, zigzagging up and down the aisles with no sense of orientation or direction. Then I spot the familiar shape of my Honda and run for cover.

I persuade Shereen to let me into her house, then into her bedroom, which is in the basement. Both of her parents are upstairs, asleep.

"I have nothing to say to you," she whispers.

Her bedroom is dark. I sit at the foot of the bed but Shereen won't join me. I watch the silhouette of her body as she paces across the floor. "Listen," I say. "I'm sorry about the party."

"That's not the issue here, Rick."

"But I am," I say, and I really am. I feel terrible.

"The issue is why you lied to me. And what you did instead."

"I just needed some time to myself," I say. "To get my thoughts together."

"Bull*shit,* Rick."

"No," I say.

"What thoughts do you have to 'get together'?"

"About us," I say.

"What about us?"

"I love you," I say, and it is God's honest truth: I love her and I want to be with her, only her, forever and ever. She is basically all I need. "You're everything I need."

"Save it."

"I'm serious." She hears the crack in my voice and sits next to me. I put my arm around her. "Can't you see it working out? Picture us in a nice house, with two kids. Can't you see it?"

Shereen studies my eyes. "I've always seen it," she finally says, letting out her breath.

"I didn't, until tonight."

"There were no girls with you?"

"No," I say, "no," and she stretches back on the bed, relieved. I lie down beside her. "Come on," I say. "Don't you think we could live that way? Like our parents are? Happy."

"I want to . . ."

I kiss her. "Then we're all set."

Shereen grabs my sides. "Listen, you," she says. "If you want it to work, you have to try."

"I know."

"You have to *want* it to work."

I slide my hands under her nightgown, up and over her breasts. She reaches around my waist and hooks her thumbs into my back pockets.

"I want it to work," I say. "Believe me, I want it to work."

And just for an instant, all the guilt vanishes and I realize that I *am* normal, that I've got nothing to worry about, that I've got a hopeful and happy life ahead of me with the love of a beautiful woman. I will never give up Shereen, not now, not ever.

Then her thumbs discover the tattered remains of my underwear, shoved into my back pocket. Shereen turns the cloth over in her hands, feeling the elastic waistband, realizing what it is even in the darkness of her basement.

"Rick—" she starts.

It's not what you think, I want to say, but I'm speechless. She reads the guilt on my face and slaps at it, hard, then slaps me again and again, shrieking and sobbing and shoving me down on her bed. I don't make any move to stop her.

"I lost him," Valerie said, turning to me with the cell phone held away from her head as we flew down Highway 27 in her Land Rover.

I nodded and said, "Well, we're way out here."

"No, Rachel, we're most of the way to Montauk," Valerie said to me as if I were her daughter instead of her cook. "The Hamptons is not 'way out here.' Friday afternoon traffic just makes you think so. Really we're less than a hundred and twenty miles out of the city."

I didn't bother reminding her that I was from Syracuse and that I had some sense of New York geography, apart from the fact that we'd been driving out to East Hampton every weekend for two months.

She brought the phone to the steering column and held it with both hands, staring at it. Her French manicure and plump pea-sized diamond looked so good and the phone and the leather steering wheel looked so impeccable that she could've been doing an ad for Motorola or Land Rover. Valerie drove with her knees while examining the phone. After about thirty seconds, she pushed her sunglasses up on top of her head and brought the phone closer to her eyes. The Land Rover continued to hurtle down the road at about ninety miles an hour.

"I can't see what light is lit on this thing," Valerie said, squinting at the phone, which was nearly touching her nose. Then she sighed an extravagant sigh and thrust the phone toward me without looking so that she nearly clocked me in the temple. "Here, you look," she said. "See if you can get Jamie back for me."

I caught the phone just as she let go and looked at the lights, which plainly read "No Svc."

"Oh. We must be between towers," I said.

"Really?" Valerie started peeking out, up from under the front windshield, as if there were a tower so near the car as to be hovering above us like a UFO.

"Could you not see the little red light here?" I said as I snapped the gray phone shut and set it on the dashboard.

"Could you not see the little red light here?" Valerie mocked me in a high-pitched cartoon whine. Then she smiled. "You're not supposed to point out your boss's shortcomings, Rachel."

"I like to think of you as a client, Valerie," I said.

"Of course you do." She smiled a magnanimous burgundy-lipped smile. Then she flipped the sunglasses back down on her nose. "There was a glare," she said. "Coming in my window. I couldn't get away from it."

And then, as if by miracle, the phone rang.

Valerie picked it up. "Baby," she cooed.

"You lost me," Jamie said.

"I hate that," Valerie said.

Valerie and Jamie hired me after Valerie's first trimester. I had been out of cooking school exactly one month when I catered a party for my older brother, who was a business associate of Jamie's. Valerie loved my gazpacho. "I haven't tasted gazpacho this good since I was in Andalusia two years ago," she said. "You're a genius."

"It's the New Jersey tomatoes," I said. "They're great this year."

She was also a particular fan of the coconut and cinnamon sorbets. "You must come work for me," she said to me in the kitchen at the end of the party. "You need a full-time job, don't you? Young chefs always need work. I can introduce you to great people. Really get your business off the ground."

I didn't bother telling her I didn't have a catering business per se, that I was just doing my brother a favor. I also didn't say I was waiting for my phone to ring with a call from Union Square, Gramercy, or Bouley saying they were looking for a sous-chef. "I'm going to be a superfamous chef" isn't exactly the thing to tell inquisitive strangers. Anyway, I had other things on my mind—namely the recent scalding failure of my planned nuptials—and wasn't likely to come up with a good response.

My fiancé and I were college sweethearts (we met sophomore year in a music 101 course nicknamed Clapping for Credit) and after graduation we survived a few years of Michigan-New York distance while Dan studied law and I attended cooking school. We resolved to come to the city, together, and rented a tiny one-bedroom walk-up in Park Slope that had a working fireplace and a view of Prospect Park, if you leaned way out over the fire escape and squinted. The apartment was quiet and smelled like my grandparents' house, or mothballs, I guess, which I liked. Dan got a job with a commercial real estate firm. I was cleaning lettuce in midtown. On weekends, we took the D train to Coney Island or watched movies or met friends in bars. Everything seemed to be going super well; we both thought so.

He proposed on Halloween, with a mood ring in a cab riding home from a party. The next morning we were at Tiffany's when the doors opened—Dan's grandfather had left him some money that he was supposed to use for his wife's engagement ring and Dan stayed true to these wishes. By Christmastime, we had set a date, deciding on October 9, fall color and crispness and all that.

It was a snowless winter and a soaking wet March. And then, the day I came home dizzy from dress shopping with my sister-in-law, Dan was too quiet and ate nothing of his favorite squash soup. In bed in the dark, I started to kiss his neck and he gently pushed me away. He said he thought we were jumping the gun, that maybe we had changed more than we thought in our years apart. He wanted to suspend the specifics ("For instance?" I said, and he replied, "Don't buy the dress yet"), and just stay engaged for a while, see how it went. But how it went was, a week later he said he'd fallen in love with the other lawyer in his office, he was sorry, but, well, he was sorry, what could he say? I set the ring back in the turquoise blue box on top of his TV, packed some clothes, my knives, and my two best saucepans, and I took a cab to my brother's. The next morning, I decided I couldn't face the arugula, so I quit and started looking for a better job.

It was during this heartbroken, angry, unemployed half-consciousness that I first spoke to Valerie. Sure, I said to her, I'd love to meet and talk about cooking privately for you. Sounds *great.*

A couple days after the party, I went to her loft above a SoHo gallery. The floors were blond wood and the whole place smelled like nothing except, vaguely, leather and wood—it was an expensive space that never got dirty or complicated or worn; no animals, no cooking, no body odor, no children. The walls were white, as were the moldings and trim. The living room windows were huge. There were some paintings that looked like a series of cloth swatches—mere black stripes on white canvas. I call such paintings "I could do that" art. My assessment was that Valerie and her husband rarely cooked in and that they had a very good cleaning lady who came twice a week. I counted twelve closets and two doors along the hallway between the front door and the living room.

All of this was fine with me, just a contrast to my new Hell's Kitchen studio, which smelled like whatever was ripening on my counter melded with starch from the Chinese dry cleaners downstairs and exhaust fumes from the Lincoln Tunnel. If I left the bathroom door open while peeing, I could touch both the front door and the kitchen cabinet. It was cozy.

She offered me an espresso or an Evian and then we sat opposite one another—me on the couch, she on a black leather chaise longe.

"My baby shouldn't be fed by my mouth," she stated right off. In response to my look of puzzlement she said, "For me it's either mac and cheese and ramen at home or oysters and foie gras out. Jamie's a good cook, but that's only dinners, and that's only sometimes. This baby needs nourishment, I suppose I do too, and the last thing I'm going to take on with this pregnancy is a lesson in being I-can-cook girl. You know?"

I nodded sagely as if I'd had so many clients hire me before for exactly the same reason. I hadn't, in fact, even known that Valerie was pregnant. So I smiled and said, "You have a problem with I-can-cook girls?"

"Oh no, I didn't mean to offend you, I just meant, well, you know." She looked to me with her hands raised, and I decided not to pursue the ridiculous comment.

Then she confessed her phobia of raw meat, and I began to write down her food principles. She said she was allergic to nothing and ate most everything, except dairy products.

"No dairy whatsoever?" I said. "So you drink soy milk, rice milk . . ." I was searching.

"No, no," she said, tossing her head back as she reclined on the chaise longe, and then arching way back so that she could look upside down out the window behind us.

I waited for her to return.

Then she sat up, stretched her arms over her head, and dropped them back in front of her and clasped her hands around her belly. "Nope. I don't drink milk."

I didn't bother to ask how she made mac and cheese. I assumed she meant the Kraft boxed kind, which calls for milk.

"And cheese?"

"Oh, I eat cheese from time to time," she said.

"Regular cheese?"

"What do you mean?" she said.

"Gouda, Swiss, Cheddar, Gruyère, Brie, Feta . . ."

"No cheese slices," she said.

"Ah-hah." I wrote this down.

"How about yogurt?"

"Frozen yes, Dannon no."

"Okay," I said. "So you do eat some dairy products."

"No," she said. "I thought I already said that. No dairy."

"But cheese and frozen yogurt . . ." I started to say, then stopped.

She was still looking straight at me, waiting to contradict whatever the end of my sentence would be.

"Okay," I said, "no dairy. Except cheese and fro yo, which are technically considered dairy."

"I don't eat dairy."

"Right."

We talked for a few hours that day. I got the whole story about her fancy casting agency just a block over, in another loft. It meant some weird hours for her, and thus for me, too. But there was a kitchen in the office—it was a big, fun, run-down space, she said, and everyone was so friendly. Lots of good-looking people, maybe I would even meet someone special. She winked at me.

"Great!" I replied, without a trace of sincerity.

"It feels like being St. Peter sometimes," Valerie said. "Just watching these people stream through and knowing you're only going to tap one or two or maybe three for an ad or movie or pilot. Anyway, I shouldn't think it will be much of an inconvenience for you to work out of both places."

As she said this, I imagined walking down Prince Street at noon on a Saturday with my arms full of pots and knives, while tourists from all parts of New York and the world packed into SoHo with hopes of either seeing someone famous, or seeming famous themselves.

"Anyway," she said, "the agency is a fun place to be around. Or I suppose it is if you aren't me and running it."

I decided not to say that I didn't plan on hanging around a lot, to meet people or otherwise, at "the agency." Nor did I say then that she'd have to provide some basic cookware at the office if I was to cook there. Instead I asked her about getting extra calcium during her pregnancy and about avoiding shellfish, both things I remembered from my sister-in-law's pregnancy. "Yeah, my doctor said something about that," she said. "I do have supplements. But she said I shouldn't count on those for my calcium."

"Uh-huh." I decided we'd get her the calcium-fortified orange juice. Spinach. Lots of brie. I kept these thoughts to myself. I learned very quickly that it was best to keep Valerie strategically uninformed. How my food tasted was all she needed to know.

When I realized that I would take the job, I was a little horrified. I didn't like Valerie and I thought I was too principled to give in to her simply because she knew famous people and had tons of dough. I was supposed to be waiting for my big break, and if it was just money I needed, I could flip burgers or clean lettuce again. But I'd be a liar to say I didn't envy her huge loft (plus the houses in East Hampton and Aspen). I'd also be lying to say it was no big deal that she called Robert DeNiro "Bob" and Martin Scorcese "Marty." She could get a table at any restaurant in town; Madonna was in her Rolodex. Still, I had hoped I was too principled.

"If this works out, you know, for both us," she said, "it could really work. I mean, even after the baby is born. My mother's not the kind of woman who'll show up and make chicken soup and lasagna to last until the baby's in training pants."

"Okay," I said. "But neither am I."

"Neither are you what?"

"The type of chef who'll come over and cook for your freezer."

"Uh-huh," Valerie said, turning and looking out her loft window at the white iron arches of the building across the street. "Persnickety, aren't you?" she said, smiling.

"Are you always this combative?" I replied.

We shook hands and made it official.

Cooking for Valerie and Jamie succeeded in getting my mind off Dan a bit. I stopped drawing pictures on his face in our college yearbook and I finally removed the pile of cut-up photographs that had become a mountain of sorts with the aid of hot wax from the candles surrounding it. I found other things to talk about with my friends. I still had the dreams at night, but then I imagined those would continue for a while, or at least I hoped, because it was only in my dreams that I was sad instead of purely furious. Usually I dreamed I was on a crowded street and I would see Dan's father or little sister across the street, waiting for a bus or cab. I would try to greet them, to get their attention, to get to them, because I wanted to say I missed them and I wanted them to tell me they were sorry for Dan's bad behavior, and that they missed me, too, really missed me. But of course the cab or bus always zipped away with them just about to turn their heads in my direction, and I was left there, alone and anonymous once again.

When we got to East Hampton that Friday, I set about organizing and preparing the weekend's food. Valerie pulled on some spandex and clipped on her utility belt—so named by me because it held both her Walkman and her cell phone—and she went walking on the beach. It was cool and foggy that day. From the kitchen window I could see only about a hundred yards into the water. Waves lapped the beach so that the surface of the water barely swayed, all at the edges.

I chopped rosemary and thyme for a roast chicken I was going to cook and then slice for sandwiches. I peeled and boiled some beets for a puree to go with the swordfish I would grill that night. And I made banana bread because Valerie loved it and she ate it with cream cheese—more calcium.

Sometimes I wished I was making a ginger-banana soufflé in a restaurant kitchen instead of sour cream banana bread in an old electric oven in East Hampton. But then, baking always soothed me—in college, my roommate would know that Dan and I had fought by the two batches of cookies she'd come home to after studying in the library all evening. Anyway, I had only been a soufflé chef for three or four years. For fourteen years prior to that, I cooked what would have been the biggest hit at Syracuse church bake sales, i.e., things involving chocolate chips, caramel cubes, sweetened condensed milk, butter, and coconut in a nine-by-thirteen-inch pan at 350 degrees Fahrenheit.

Of course when I got to feeling as if I were losing my skills, it was always my option to whip up a little batch of petit fours or a perfect foie gras for Valerie and Jamie. They loved eating things that they had to pronounce with an accent. Yet what I found most satisfying about cooking for them was my victory in the calcium battle with "no-dairy" Valerie. The second day of our contract, I made her a banana-strawberry yogurt shake for breakfast and she requested them every day thereafter. Nothing was ever said about the fact that I used milk and nonfrozen yogurt in the concoction—she loved it so I continued to make it.

"It's all you," Valerie said to me that morning while drinking a shake before we left for East Hampton. I was doing dishes. "It's your cooking that's keeping me so healthy."

"I'd love to think that, Val," I replied. "But some people just get lucky and have really easy pregnancies." She'd had virtually no troubles and she was six months gone. Her feet swelled during the day and every now and then she'd get a zit the size of China. But there was no nausea, no out-of-control cravings, no sleeplessness, even. I was thankful for this—maybe as thankful as she was.

"Well, all I know is that my pregnancy would be a lot harder without you."

"Thanks," I said, a little shocked at the compliment. She was rarely direct—usually it was some backhanded compliment that old, grumpy men excelled at, like, "Are you sure I'm getting my money's worth?" Or, my personal favorite, "You went to that big school for this?"

To these jabs, I easily replied, "Terminate this contract any time you like, Valerie. I'll take my Cuisinart and Calphalon elsewhere." It became a routine, calling one another's bluff time and time again.

Thus, to her huge and unusual compliment that morning, I had only been able to reply, "Do you want chicken or lamb for lunch?"

The baby kicked then, and Valerie pretty much shrieked with excitement. She grabbed my dishwater-wet hands and pressed it against her belly. I felt a little bit of aftershock as if the baby were pulling the covers back up around its shoulders after it had rolled onto its tummy.

"Do you think Jamie will make a good father?" she asked.

I immediately wondered if she'd snuck a couple of beers when I wasn't looking. I was shocked. I also didn't know Jamie that well. So I stuttered for a moment, fought against the smart-ass response.

"He'll be fantastic," I said finally. "So will you."

"Good," she said. "I really hope so."

The fact was, neither one of them would be parents to whom I would relate. I grew up the daughter of a writer and a professor in Syracuse. My mother worked, sure; she taught classes and wrote books and articles. But she was also home with me and my brother full-time. She cooked meatloaf and mashed potatoes and she hand-pitted cherries and made a pie crust from scratch while supporting Roe v. Wade. This is to say that she was far from being a stereotypical housewife, yet she stayed home with me and my brother. She was a mother first.

"Mother first" did not seem to be what Valerie had in mind. I knew because she had already talked about it, a lot. That her baby would have a nanny from the get-go. That it would eat sushi by age five and would spend more money on tuition by the time it was eight than I'd spent in four years at a ridiculously expensive private college. The kid would probably be in summer camp for eight weeks a summer and boarding school for seven months a year. I wasn't willing to say that any of these things were bad per se because they were completely out of my realm of experience.

Dusk in East Hampton. Valerie was still walking the beach and I was holding a big swordfish steak when the phone rang.

"Rache," Jamie said. "What's up?"

"Marinating," I said.

"Sounds good." Jamie was hollering a little bit; he sounded far away, or like he was about to go out of range.

"Where are you?"

"Far. Maybe another hour and a half."

"Traffic?"

"Does it rain in a rain forest?"

"Right," I said. "Although, not really."

"Val there?" he asked.

"She's on the beach. Walking," I said, dropping the swordfish into the big pyrex pan where a lime-honey-sesame marinade was waiting.

"Thanks, I'll get her there," he said.

Five minutes later, Valerie trucked into view. She was doing her "speed walk" arm swing that her trainer had taught her, but just with one arm. Her other hand held the phone. One side of her Walkman headphones were pushed back so that the phone could get to her ear. I imagined Jamie getting a whiff of Salt-n-Pepa and Courtney Love as Val talked to him and continued her workout.

As she turned up the beach and approached the deck, I could see that she was upset. Her finely plucked dark eyebrows were squinched together and her lips were moving fast and tight. Just as she was about to step up onto the deck and come inside, she stopped. She glanced up at the house all lit up, and then she turned and sat down on the sand right in front. Because of her belly size, she had to squat until she almost reached the ground, and then she sort of fell back onto the sand.

I popped a beer and continued to think about Dan—would he and the lawyer he fell for make it? I wondered, as I did often those days, what had been wrong about us, or wrong about me. I had never let him tell me anything but that he was in love with this other woman—I figured that if he wanted to dump me, he could live with never getting to explain himself. He could live with my hating him, with not getting my understanding or my forgiveness. It was, I figured, the least he could do.

But he had called that morning, catching me on the way out the door as I was headed to Valerie's.

"What can I do for you?" I said. "I'm running off to work."

Dan was caught a little off guard. "Oh—sorry. Yeah, your brother told me about your gig with the casting agent. Sounds great. Could be just the connection you need to hit the big time."

"Could be I don't need any connection," I said. "Thanks."

"Okay," Dan said. "Sorry to have caught you at a bad time."

I kept going: "My brother had no right telling you about my life."

Dan paused, then said, "I'll call some other time."

I didn't respond, but trilled my fingers on my kitchen counter. I wished I had long nails so that they would click and he would hear them.

Dan still didn't hang up. He said, "You're being pretty harsh, you know?"

"And I'm supposed to be how?"

"Whatever," Dan said. "I'll talk to you later." He hung up.

I suppose I was satisfied, and I really did feel good for a split second. But then I was sobbing and I didn't so much feel triumphant and satisfied as utterly alone. I wailed facedown on my bed. I cried well past the point when your stomach and throat ache, when it feels like you've been throwing up.

Then I got up, showered again, and got to Valerie's an hour late. I told her there was a water main break in Times Square, that I had to walk up to 55th Street and take the N to the 4 train at 53rd and Lex. She believed this. "Start taking cabs," she said. "I'll pay your fare—the subway is disgusting. You can get pinkeye or molested down there. Worst of all—it's unreliable. It can screw up your whole day."

Standing in East Hampton twelve hours later, I decided I must be on the road to recovery after such a big breakdown. It was a turning point. Maybe Valerie had been right—maybe I should start keeping my eyes peeled at the agency.

When she finally came in from the beach, it was dark out. The banana bread was cooling on the counter and the swordfish was marinating in the fridge.

"I've lost him," Val said, setting the cell phone down on the table and unbuckling her Walkman belt, which sat below her belly like the waistbands on large men.

I looked at the clock on the microwave. They must've been on the phone for nearly an hour and a half. "He should be here pretty soon, shouldn't he? Another hour at most?"

"No, I've really lost him. He's on his way back to the city."

The phone rang again.

"You answer it," she said.

I froze for a moment until Valerie lifted the phone from its receiver and put it up to my ear.

"Hello?" I said as she held it there.

"Rache. It's me. Tell Val, that—" He paused. "Tell her—"

"Uh-huh?" I said, having no other choice. I looked into Valerie's anxious and insistent face and I took over holding the phone to my ear. She stepped back and then turned to pour herself a glass of water. She drank it with one hand on her hip, still facing away from me.

"Tell her that she's beautiful and that we'll be great parents and that I didn't mean what I said about hating cartoons, fairs, circuses, zoos, Barney, playgrounds, and anything else 'kid related.' Just tell her that, okay?" Then he hung up.

"Umm," I said, more awkward than I could believe, looking at Valerie's swayed back. "He said to tell you that you're beautiful and that he didn't mean what he said about zoos, circuses, Barney, Sesame Street, and jungle gyms."

Val slowly set her glass down on the counter and turned to face me. "He said he hated everything with the word 'kid' in it and he wondered if we were doing the right thing," Valerie said. She started walking out of the kitchen. "He's gone. He's history."

I didn't bother putting my two cents in, that it seemed like a perfectly normal fear to be having, despite the horrendous manner he was choosing to express it. I wasn't their counselor, after all. I was just their cook. I opened a second beer and shucked a couple ears of corn.

Valerie showered for a long time. When she reemerged from the bathroom, I was sitting on the couch reading *Entertainment Weekly*, wondering if Dan had called looking for forgiveness and for us to try and be friends or some old bullshit; or whether he had dumped the lawyer and wanted me back. (Hah! I thought.) Val got a glass of juice from the fridge and joined me on the couch. She seemed surprisingly calm, given her husband's choice words and the tantrum they produced not so long ago. Her dark hair was wet and pulled back in a rubber band. She had on her maternity jeans and an old sweater that had holes in the elbows.

"You know, there are lots of different ways to raise children," she said, dropping the magazine to her lap. "People get all proprietary about it. Knowing the right way. I'm going to do a great job bringing up this kid." She took a long drink of juice and I sat listening, reassuring myself that my jaw had not dropped. She spoke quietly, as if it was a real voice from somewhere below her bottom rib that was speaking, for the first time in a very long while. What had coaxed this Valerie out of hiding?

"For instance, I know you're horrified when I talk about nannies and preschool tuitions. When the simple matter is, you didn't grow up that way. So you don't know that it can work."

I nodded. I liked the beginning of what she said—she almost seemed real—but I didn't like that she was now using me as a comparison.

Valerie continued: "And I bet the first French you ever spoke was in high school, am I right?"

I nodded.

"My baby is going to be bilingual from the time it's three because we're going to have a French-speaking Nanny. What do you think?" Valerie did her best to seem unaware of having semi-insulted me.

"Great," I said. "Sounds great." I looked back at the clock on the oven. 8:41 P.M. I chuckled to myself at how unsubtle she'd been in saying that her kid would be a lot smarter and more sophisticated than me. "Yeah," I almost added. "And she or he will be a lot more fucked up than me, too, from having a psycho power-monger mother." I couldn't say this, much as I would've liked to, but I had to say something. So I blurted, "My French is pretty good, by the way."

"Oh, I'm sure it is. But starting young is the best thing, really." Valerie reached for my beer with a smug little grin on her face. "I need a little taste," she said. "Maybe I'll have a whole one with you, and skip having wine with my husband, who may or may not show up."

"Mais, bien sûr," I cooed.

She leaned back and put her feet up on the glass coffee table. A wind came in off the water through the screen door and blew a piece of that day's *Times* onto the floor. Wind was coming from the south. Fog would blow away or burn off by morning, hopefully. I wondered what Valerie was like before she was successful, If she was ever consistently nice and relaxed and normal before she spent her days with all the freak actors and anorexic models and the agents who drove them. If I became Namebrand Superchef, what would I be like?

"Jamie will come around. But he'll have to do it on his own," she said with her eyes closed. "When we should probably be doing it together. I have his questions, too, you know? We're going to be parents together. We should be able to work this out together." She opened her eyes as she thought of something else. "Do we, by any chance, have any Cheetos? I have a mean craving for Cheetos."

"How lowbrow of you," I said as I stood up. I went and retrieved an unopened bag from my backpack. Cheetos were my weakness, too, but I didn't tell her that. Valerie looked so gleeful that I half-expected her to clap her hands together and say, "Oh boy," as I tossed the unopened bag to her. Instead she caught the bag, grinned broadly, and said, "Excellent."

"Now, what about you, Miss Rachel," Valerie said. "You're always so mysterious about your love life. Is there anyone?"

I took a long swallow of beer and formed the words in my head before I said them. "My fiancé broke off our engagement several months ago, right before I started to cook for you."

"God, Rachel," she said. "That's really awful. I am so, so sorry."

"Well, I don't particularly like to talk about it." I laughed nervously because it suddenly felt good to talk about it, to let Valerie know what I thought about while whisking eggs or cream or peeling vegetables for her. Maybe I also wanted to let her know that she didn't have a monopoly on the trials and tribulations of the world around her.

Valerie crunched a handful of Cheetos. Then she said, "But you've got to talk about it. It's the only way to make sense of it."

"I thought we were set, you know?" I said before I could stop myself. "I thought I knew my life. Our life."

"Everyone thinks that once or twice. Everyone has to go through something like this. You'll make it," Valerie said, stretching her arms over her head. "Of course, for the moment, I'm sure it sucks and I'm sorry." This last bit was said mid-stretch, to the ceiling.

I got up and went to the screen door, thinking that I didn't need Valerie to tell me that my problems were average piss, rite-of-passage sort of problems. I coughed to hold onto the composure I was finally losing. I kept staring out the screen door, into the darkness. For one brief moment I thought, "Maybe she's right. In her own pathetic little way, maybe she's right." That's when I spotted Jamie. Standing to the side of the deck, just out of the light spilling from the kitchen. He was watching her—I could tell by the way he was staring in through the window. He didn't see me.

Suddenly I loved them both like they were my siblings or parents. I felt pathetic for this, and maybe pathetic for disliking them in the first place. But I also knew that I'd dislike them again, soon even, when Valerie had a tantrum with the delivery boy while Kevin Costner was on hold, or when Jamie told me how much he'd made in stocks last month. And I'd probably hate them again for having each other.

"Should we eat, chef?" she said to my back. "I'm not willing to wait for him any longer."

I nodded and watched Jamie watching her, staring at her, really, with this mournful, longing look on his face. I couldn't tell Valerie he was there; but I also couldn't take my eyes off him. It was creepy, and beautiful. Then he picked up his cell phone, tiny blue flip thing, and the phone rang in the kitchen. I looked back at Valerie, she looked at me, then finally stood up to get it. She didn't say anything after "hello" and just turned her face toward the wall. Outside, I could see Jamie's mouth moving as he still watched her through the window.

So I slipped out the front door and around the other side of the house from where I'd seen Jamie, and I walked onto the beach. The sand was cool and a little bit clammy beneath my feet. It seemed like it might rain before morning; I wasn't sure anymore that the fog would blow away.

I walked down a couple houses until there was one with no lights on. Then I walked up to the edge of the dune grass and lay down. Clouds were thick but there were intermittent star-filled patches like cleared spots in a steamed mirror. I imagined they'd probably made up by now and were weeping together on the couch, Jamie with his hand under Valerie's shirt, cupped around the bottom of her stomach.

Anyway, I was thinking that the bottom line didn't have much to do with Valerie and Jamie, or, even, Dan. I was having a moment of total clarity right then and I felt sure I'd realize something very important and helpful. Maybe I was about to truly believe that Dan and I just weren't meant to be and that I should see the present breakup as a whole lot less painful than what might've happened five years down the road. Or maybe it was that Dan and I were destined to be, and I should forgive him and do anything it took to get him back. Or maybe it was that I should move to a new city and start over, leaving them all behind—Dan, Valerie, Jamie, the lawyer girl, and the restauranteurs who hadn't hired me yet.

But just as I was reaching for one of these certainties, the clarity disappeared with the rest of the stars. I worked back through to that point of clarity, trying to stay precise, exact, to get that almost-conclusion back.

But then, I pretty much failed. I gave up and fell asleep.

I awoke when I heard Jamie calling for me. By the clamminess of my skin and the sleepiness of my eyes, I knew I must've slept for an hour or two. I stood and saw him walking down the beach, having already passed me. "Jamie—" I said in a half-shout. "Here I am."

He turned, saw me walking toward him. "There you are," he said. "We thought we lost you."

MOTHER

Aisha D. Gayle

We were lying in my bed, side by side. Outside, the first blizzard of the season raged, but I was surrounded by comfort. The big golden lion that Chris had given me for Christmas was underneath my head. My mother lay back against my maroon headrest. We were curled underneath my comforter with the dark green vines and blooming flowers that were different shades of red. Above the mahogany dresser that stood in front of my bed, cluttered with cream-colored candles, jewelry boxes, and school pictures of my friends, I could see us in the mirror. My mother was holding the koala bear I had had since forever, plucking at its worn fur. A stuffed monkey sat between us, the words *Planet Hollywood* written on his T-shirt, a memento of the time she suddenly decided one day last summer to take me to see *Miss Saigon,* and we ate out and pretended we were best friends. There was a night table standing on either side of us—one side held my alarm clock, a bible, and my telephone; the other held a ceramic jar with a yellow baby duck on the front of it, my blue book of poems, and my black Bic mechanical pencil with the purple clip.

"Mommy?"

"Hmmm?" She left my koala bear momentarily, her hand reaching out to grab one of my braids.

I blurted it out quickly. "I got a sixty-three on my Physics test."

"Did you study?"

"Not hard enough, apparently."

"Eyes on the prize, girl. Eyes on the prize," she murmured. I hissed out air between my teeth. I hated her inspirational phrases. We would yell at each other, she'd always get the last word, and it'd be something like "Attitude plus aptitude equals altitude," or "Persistence and perseverance."

"I hate Dr. Morgan."

"No, you don't."

"Fine, then I hate physics."

"Attitude is ninety-nine percent of the battle. 'I think I can' is the key to—"

"I feel fat."

"Now what did I tell you about image of self? If you like who you are, then others—"

"I'm not going to get into college."

"Baby, you have to sell yourself. Believe—"

"Chris and I aren't talking."

"In any relationship, the silences are just as important as—"

"I think . . . PMS."

"Oh, well . . . that's that then." I hated the tears that were inexplicably clotting on my eyelashes and rolling their way, unwillingly, down the sides of my face, toward my ears. She dug her arm underneath my back, around my shoulders, and folded me into her side, understanding bad days. She felt soft and strong under my cheek, her skin warm, her round body making the perfect cushion. There is nothing in the world like the feel of a mother beside you, there with you, absorbing your tears and never failing to make them her own. I cried.

I was in the passenger seat of our van, my friends in the seats behind me. It was around one in the morning and my mother was driving everybody back to our boarding school. We had been at my best friend's surprise sweet sixteen party. My mother was staring out at the road. Like so many other nights. I fell asleep.

I lazily opened my eyes what must've been a few minutes later. I could hear my mother mumbling to herself. I narrowed my eyes at her, turned my head, looked outside. There was nothing but a few garbage bags lining the side of the highway. Slightly puzzled but no longer interested, I fell back asleep.

When I awoke we were at school, and everyone was climbing out.

"Thanks, Mrs. Richards."

"Good-night, Mrs. Richards."

"Thanks, Ms. Richards."

One of my friend's mothers, Mrs. Cummings, pulled her van near ours and waved. My mother unlocked our car doors, stepped out, and walked over to her.

"Hey, Mom, what're you doing?" She didn't answer. I got out of the car and went over to my mother and Mrs. Cummings. My mother was sobbing, huge hysterical gulps. I'd never seen my mother cry before. "What's wrong with you?" I asked, confused.

"Yanique, go call your father and tell him he has to come pick your mother up." Mrs. Cummings spoke in a low, soothing tone, but her eyes showed her worry. She flagged over my friend Tara's father. I ran into the dormitory, scared, and called my dad. He sighed, said he was on his way.

"What's the matter with her, Daddy?" There were tears in the back of my throat, making it hard to swallow past them.

"I don't know." He hung up. I climbed down the stairs, numbly, afraid to go back and find her still crying. My dorm master stopped me in the hall, squeezed my shoulder, told me she understood.

I found my mother sitting in the hallway of Clinton, holding tightly to Mrs. Cummings and Mr. Wycoff. She wasn't really crying anymore, but a dry sobbing sound came out of her mouth—the noise was somehow empty, more painful to hear without the tears that were supposed to accompany the pain.

"Mommy?" She looked at me, looked through me.

"Yanique, we've got her. Why don't you go outside and wait for your father?" I nodded, walked out. I didn't want to be alone. The cold air, which I hadn't really noticed until now, eased its way inside my jacket to wait with me. I sat down on the bench outside . . . waited. Wrapped my arms around my stomach for warmth, around the back of my neck in frustration, and finally around my head to hold myself together. I was scared to be alone.

He laid a hand on my shoulder and I jumped. When I turned, I saw Erik and I almost began echoing the sobs of my mother. He wasn't my boyfriend, he was my best friend. It wasn't until afterward . . . not till after he stood in front of me shivering, his favorite tie-dyed Grateful Dead T-shirt peaking out from under his down jacket . . . not till after I saw his worried eyes looking into mine, his hands reaching out to comfort, then falling back, unsure . . . not till afterward that I realized how much more I needed his—

"Yani? Tara came to get me. She said—"

"My mom . . ." And then I began to feel guilty—for wanting to give him a problem that belonged to me, a problem that I inherently knew was supposed to be a secret. No one was supposed to know that my mother had looked through me.

So I stood up and into Erik's arms, trying to cry, trying to force this hurt, this confusion, this bewilderment upward, out of my body. The tears wouldn't come. I simply hiccuped, told him I didn't know what was happening, and asked him to stop the numbness. I couldn't say any more. Didn't have to. He held me. His hand made circles on my back while the other held my hand, and he told me stories to make me smile. But I wanted my mom.

"You're father is here." Erik nudged me up from his shoulder, then quietly slipped away.

"Should I take her to the hospital?" my father asked when I saw him.

"I don't know . . . I think so?" *I'm only fifteen. This has never happened before. How do I know what to do? You're the father.*

"I'm taking her to the hospital." This was a statement. I nodded, relieved.

"Take her to Clearview," I said.

"Muhlenburg is closer."

"She wouldn't want to go to Muhlenburg."

We thanked Mrs. Cummings and Mr. Wycoff. "She talked about you, you know. I know you think she didn't see you, but all she talked about was you." I couldn't manage "thank you," so I nodded at Mr. Wycoff's statement. They drove away.

My mother wouldn't get in the car. She wailed low in her throat, like women in a long line on their way to a funeral. "Bodies . . . ," she'd whimper. My dad finally coaxed her in half an hour later. I sat in the backseat, clutching my hands together. Then she started. These god-awful keening noises, over and over again, a litany, a chant of some-one in mortal hell, as my dad put the car into reverse. I tucked myself into myself, put my arms around my head, and squeezed my eyes shut, but I could still hear her. My dad held her hand with one of his and drove with his other. She moaned over, and over, and over.

We got to the hospital and they made us sit at this small little desk and answer too many questions.

"Primary health care?" Who cares? My mother isn't my mother any-more, please take her and make her better. They put her in an exam-ining room. Everything was white. The bedsheets were white. The cab-inets were white. The gloves were white. The Q-Tips were white. My dad looked at me worriedly.

"You should try and sleep."

"Where?" I asked humorlessly. We waited.

And waited.

"Let me see if I can find you a place to sleep."

"Daddy, no, it's really okay, I—" He took off. I pitied him. He needed something, anything, to do. Minutes later I was following a nurse to a stretcher of my own.

"I wear contacts." Which were now residing in a permanent place on my corneas. The nurse smiled (*why was she smiling?*), left, came back with two containers for my lenses. I followed her to the bathroom, then went back to my stretcher. Everything was fuzzy now. I could no longer see distinct shapes and expressions, and I was glad I wouldn't have to see the look of pity on that nurse's face. I sat on the edge of the stretcher. My dad came in.

"Sleep," he said.

"I don't want to." He came over and pushed me down gently. I sat back up. "I don't want to." He wrung his hands. I'd never seen my father wring his hands before. He left. I finally heard the doctor's voice. I don't remember his voice. He asked my mother questions. He examined her. He admitted her.

My mother, father, and I followed someone out of the emergency room and down the hall. We turned left, then right, then left again. We passed under a sign that read BEHAVIORAL HEALTH. I didn't want to go under that sign. She was quiet.

The lights were dim. Everybody's voice was hushed. My mother had to sign herself in.

"If someone were to call, do we have permission to tell them you're here?"

My mother listened attentively. They had to repeat themselves. "No," she said.

"But, Mommy, how will we talk to you?" She looked at me, apologetic. So apologetic and frightened.

"No," she whispered.

"But what if I have to talk to you?"

"Yani, stop," my father mumbled. My shoulders drooped, my body sagged, and I began to cry. *But what if I need you?*

I fell asleep in the car on the way home. If I had been younger—if he had been younger—my father would've carried me upstairs. As it was, he tried to help me.

"I'm okay, Daddy."

"Are you hungry?" He tried so hard, and I wanted to cry again. It's not your fault.

"Could I have an Egg McMuffin?" He almost ran out of the house.

I went upstairs to my room and curled underneath the comforter. I stared at my koala bear, remembering her hands playing over it. I wanted to blame her, I wanted to save her, but all I could do was cry. This time she was not there.

RESPIRATION

Chandra Steele

You could see the hill through a clearing of trees that were leafless even though it was summer. The house, with its uneven, exposed foundation, shrugged down the hill. The shingles were like the teeth of the house's residents—yellowed and either missing or on the verge of falling out. On the arid, rocky soil was an assortment of furniture—an orange and gold sofa with its innards exposed, a drawerless chest of drawers, rusted folding chairs that no longer folded, and a nubby once-avocado armchair. Hollow aluminum poles were jabbed into the ground all over the hill. Openings had been sliced through them near the tops for ropes as bumpy and slimy as sheepgut. Inexplicably, there was a rotting pig's head on a stake at the bottom of the hill. There were kids and chickens everywhere.

Annie got out of her white car. She stepped carefully to what was meant to pass as a front door but was really a plywood plank attached to hinges. She knocked, swinging the door open to reveal a dark interior that she only got a glimpse of as the door swung back at her.

"Hello? Is anyone home?" And then, with doubt in her voice, "Mrs. McCurdle?"

Just then Annie heard an inhuman squeal that chilled her despite the heat that made her clothes adhere to her skin.

Annie saw the children freeze guiltily near her car as she turned to ask them if their mother was home. "Excuse me," she said, but she wasn't sure they heard her, so she stepped closer. They were covered in a film of dust and their hair was clumpy with filth and sweat. She began, "Is . . ." But a pack stealthiness had crept over them and they took off in one sudden motion for the scraggly trees.

"Don't mind 'em," Annie heard a wheezy voice say behind her. "They ain't much used to folk comin' 'round here."

She turned to see a heavyset woman with coarse, sparse hair wiping her hands on a housedress that didn't look like it would be much help in cleaning them.

"I didn't hear ya come. I was 'round back butcherin' a pig." Her hands took a last swipe across her dress, the pig's blood streaks fading into the worn print. "You from the agency?"

"Yes. Yes, I am," Annie said, as much for her own benefit as for Mrs. McCurdle's. She felt the need to establish herself as separate from the surroundings. "I'm Annie Ballard." She reflexively began to extend her hand, but instead made a motion to shift the bag on her shoulder. "And you must be Lucy McCurdle."

"Yes'm, I am." Mrs. McCurdle's eyes narrowed slightly. Annie realized that she hadn't been as subtle as she thought when she shifted her bag rather than shake the woman's hand. Either that or she had underestimated Mrs. McCurdle's intelligence. Both thoughts made Annie uncomfortable and she blushed slightly. She coughed nervously at the silence as the other woman surveyed her. "You bes' come in."

Annie followed Mrs. McCurdle through the plywood door into a kitchen that was in no better condition than anything else around it. Mrs. McCurdle motioned Annie to one of the mismatched chairs that surrounded a battered linoleum table.

"Coffee?" Mrs. McCurdle said as she filled a pot with water from the sink, the shaking and squeaking pipes echoing through the house.

"No, thank you."

"Suit yourself."

Annie felt uncomfortable in the house, subject to the mercies of Mrs. McCurdle. But she was there for a purpose and the sooner she got the papers signed, the sooner she could erase the smell of the place from her nostrils and her mind. She opened her bag and took out a manila folder that was thick with the papers that defined Mrs. McCurdle to the state.

"Mrs. McCurdle," she said to get the other woman's attention away from the pot on the stove. Mrs. McCurdle didn't turn around. Annie continued, "Mrs. McCurdle, as you know, we have been paying for your daughter's care for these past eleven years."

"Have *you* now?" She shifted her bulk and fixed Annie with one eye.

Annie caught her meaning but proceeded.

"Yes, *we* have." She fixed Mrs. McCurdle with her own look. "And what I am here to inform you about is that a change in the law now makes you ineligible for that aid. The monthly visits from the home health care worker will be discontinued and the medical equipment that the state has provided must be paid for or returned . . ."

For the first time that morning, Annie saw Mrs. McCurdle's stoniness begin to crumble. She slumped like a punching bag that deflates after being hit one too many times. Mrs. McCurdle turned the gas off and shuffled over to a chair near Annie. Annie moved back slightly. The smell of Mrs. McCurdle in a room with the windows shut was more than she could take.

Annie removed some forms and brochures from the folder and pushed them toward Mrs. McCurdle.

"There are some programs that you can apply for that might pay for some of her care, but you will be responsible for most of it."

Mrs. McCurdle licked her cracked lips and let out a sigh. She shifted in her chair. "We don't have no money to pay for Sally's care. I stay home with the chil'ren, and my husban', well, Joe takes off from time to time to look for work. Lord knows where he is now."

"I'm sorry, Mrs. McCurdle. You do own this house and you have an income from the pigs and chickens you sell, so your daughter is not eligible for coverage under the new law."

Mrs. McCurdle digested this and looked as though she were going to speak again when a faint choking sound came from upstairs.

"I gotta go check on her," she mumbled. She placed her hands on the table, hoisted herself up, and left the room. Annie heard her footsteps on the stairs.

Alone in the kitchen, Annie could hear the children in the woods and the pigs snuffling outside. Five minutes passed. Then ten. Annie had had enough. She craved a shower and an icy drink. She got up, slung her bag on her shoulder, and picked up the papers. She went to the stairs and called for Mrs. McCurdle. Not getting an answer, she decided to go up, which was not an easy task since some of the stairs were missing.

When Annie reached the top, she found Mrs. McCurdle in a narrow room. Before Annie even entered, she could hear the sound of assisted breathing. She hated the thought of facing what was in that room with Mrs. McCurdle, but there was no turning back now since Mrs. McCurdle had undoubtedly heard her. Mrs. McCurdle was fumbling with the covers on the hospital bed next to her. Annie dragged her eyes to look.

The girl was covered in worn, but clean, blankets that couldn't hide how wasted away she was by her neuromuscular disorder. Her skin was waxy and sallow. Her dark hair was cut short with unevenly shaped bangs, but it looked as though someone brushed it regularly. Most of her face was obstructed by the tubes that kept her alive. Her eyes were closed and Annie knew from the case file that the girl had been comatose almost from birth. How she had survived for her eleven years like this was not something Annie wanted to think about.

"Pretty much like this since the day she was born," Mrs. McCurdle said. "I knew somethin' was wrong when I had her in me, but what could I do? One thing I did do, though, was make sure this one was born proper—at a hospital, with a doctor. I heard that they can't jus' turn you away, insurance or no insurance, at the county hospital if you're with child. So I went down there with Joe when I felt her comin'.

"They didn't look none too happy to take me; no sir, they didn't, but they had to. Put me on a metal table with one nurse and a doctor who didn't look any older than what he was deliverin'. 'Push,' was all he said to me. But I barely had to. Sally jus' slid right out.

"The doc, he had a horrible face when he saw her. Like I said, he was a young 'un and I guess he couldn't stomach it. She was scrawny as could be and didn't let out no cry. The nurse went to find another doc and they took my baby away from me. All's I could see was her black hair stickin' up and her eyes squeezed tight.

"The other doc came and then they called Joe into the room. They told us Sally—I had it set in my mind to call her that soon's I laid eyes on her—was gonna have to be hooked up to some tubes and they was gonna test her. Joe jus' stood stock still and nodded his head. I asked what was wrong and they told me they wasn't quite sure yet, but they thought Sally's muscles and brain wasn't workin' right. I cried. I knew somethin' was wrong since she was in me but I still cried when they tol' me.

"But I made my mind up to keep her and take care of her. She's my own and I didn't think it right to give her away to be someone else's problem. They wheeled me into a hallway and left me there. Overcrowdin' they said. Beds are for rich people is what they meant. But I didn't mind. I jus' wanted to look at Sally. Joe came over and asked if I was okay, then he said he was goin' out for a smoke. Didn't come back from that smoke till at least a week later.

"After a day they sent me home, but Sally stayed in the hospital. I visited whenever I could but I wasn't 'lowed to hold her. She was all taped up and had tubes comin' out of her every which way. After 'bout a month, they said she could come home but she'd need to still be hooked up and a nurse'd have to come in to look after her. I told 'em I had no money, but I guess they already knew that. They sent a woman and she had me sign some papers. I didn't know what I signed and I didn't care. I was just happy my baby was comin' home.

"They brought her to the house in an ambulance. I had fixed this room up for her. Painted them rabbits on the wall myself. All the other kids is together in one room, but my Sally, she's got her own. The nurse came every day in the beginnin' to take care of her and I done my part, too.

"But Sally hasn't but once so much as opened her eyes. I don't even know what color they are. I like to think they're blue, like mine. She hasn't ever spoke a word. A noise here and there. It ain't been much of a life for her, but I done my best. Maybe if I had some money I coulda done more for her, but I don't, so I didn't. No sense in cryin' bout it now."

Mrs. McCurdle stiffened up and faced Annie. She had a look that if Annie had to put a name on she would call resolute.

"Might as well give me those papers to sign."

Annie didn't know what to say, so she mutely pulled them from the pile and handed them over with the pen she'd had at the ready since she entered the house. Mrs. McCurdle signed at all the x's and turned back to her child. Annie watched her gently stroke Sally's head with her raw, beefy hands.

Annie walked down the stairs as quietly as she could manage and left through the back door since it was the fastest way out. From an open window, she heard the metallic, unmistakable sound of an oxygen tank being turned off. Then there was a squeal almost identical to the one she heard when she arrived, but she knew it didn't come from any pig this time.

Annie knew what had just transpired upstairs as sure as if she had seen it. She froze, but the desperate need to leave thawed her and she took off, tripping over a bucket of pig's blood. She scrambled up, fumbled for her keys, and ran for her car. She flung open the door—red streaks marring the white paint, started the car, and sped off down the hill and onto the road. But she only got about a quarter of a mile before she had to pull over. Her vision was blinded by tears. Annie rubbed her eyes with her sticky hands and shook with soundless sobs.

A FORTUNE

Joy Monica T. Sakaguchi

It was a Sunday when I saw the kid and the man with the bulging wallet. I remember because Sunday was usually the only day that I don't work. Not for religious reasons . . . well, maybe it is. I don't go to church, but I do need a day of rest just like everyone else.

I started pickpocketing when I was only five. That's when Pop first showed me how easy it is for a small kid to get his tiny hand inside a man's coat without even touching the material. By the time I was seven I had an easy time snatching people's wallets right from beneath their damn noses. I used to save the wallets until I saw my pop once a month and then shove them in his hands. Boy would he yell at me.

"Hey, stupid, how many times I gotta tell you not to keep the wallets? Whatcha gonna tell your ma if she finds them? That your old man's got you stealing for him?" Then he would proceed to whisk the green bills from the thin partitions. Usually he would hand me a couple of bills and I would absently stuff them in my sock without counting it. Of course I should have counted the money. I just didn't want to know how much Pop thought I was worth.

My ma tried to raise me well. I have to give her credit for trying to make me an honest boy. She's this ugly lady who wears a black curly wig and cries constantly. I only call her ugly—and only I can—because I inherited her looks. Crooked teeth, oily hair, and bony knees are my curses.

I remember she cried a lot because she was always worried that I would turn out like my "stinking, rotting, lout-of-a-father." I never could figure out who she wanted me to turn out like. Uncle Barney? The only job that I ever knew he had was working as Santa Claus once a year. It's not like he was any good at it either. Good ol' Barney couldn't walk straight thanks to the flask of whiskey he kept hidden inside his red Santa suit. He once told me that the pillow he had to wear was like a shelf for his liquor. What did I know? I stopped getting excited at the sight of Santa Claus walking through our trailer door when I was five and Santa pulled off his beard and asked me to get him a stiff drink.

So I've pretty much been pickpocketing all my life; even after my old man skipped town without so much as a damn note or phone call for his only son. I don't keep the wallets anymore, but I do keep the cash. Literally. I have this huge cardboard box full of money that I have hidden in the room I rent. I don't know how much is in there, but it's a helluva lot. One day Pop will show up again. I'll hand him the boxful of money, he will throw me some bills, and then I'll just stow them away without counting them. That's what I think.

Like I said, it was a Sunday when I saw this man and his son walking around an outdoor fish market. I'd just had a meal across the street at a Chinese restaurant. The food there sucks but they're pretty generous with their fortune cookies. It's like they have to make up for the lousy food by burying their customers in cookies and all the packets of soy sauce you can carry. That's fine by me. I love those stupid fortune cookies. Today mine read, "A change in your daily routine will lead you to treasure." I memorized it and shoved it in the back pocket of my faded camouflage pants. I like to read them to my ma when I visit her at the trailer, but she usually doesn't get it. She always thinks I'm trying to tell her she was a bad mother. I don't know where she gets ideas like that. I just want to share my fortune.

The kid caught my eye first for some reason. He was about seven, and he wore a blue cap that covered most of his neatly trimmed blond hair. He followed his dad quietly. Almost too quietly for a kid his age. From the moment I saw him I felt that there was something familiar about him. His dad was one of those really yuppie-looking guys with thin hair covering his head. He wore a stiff white shirt, loose jeans, and loafers with no socks. His back pocket was bulging with the promise of greens, so even though it was Sunday, I followed them.

I stayed close, but not too close, as he went from fish to fish with the boy at his heels. Every so often the father would turn to the boy and yell at him.

"My god, Jeremy, can't you keep your damned shoes tied for five minutes?" he would say, or, "You stay close to me. I don't want to have to go looking for you if you decide to wander away." The kid just kept his eyes down and did as his father asked.

My opportunity to filch the wallet came when the kid dropped the bag he was carrying and three large salmons slipped out of their wrapping and onto the floor. The father bent over and pinched the boy's arm. "You stupid, clumsy—! Do you know how much that cost!" He hissed some other things, kind of low so that no one else could hear, just like those yuppie parents tend to do.

The way he was bending caused the wallet to peer out of his pocket and stick straight up in the air. This one would be easy. I moved real close and pretended to inspect some fish piled on a mountain of ice. With my left hand I swiftly eased out the eelskin wallet. He never noticed a thing. I took one last look at the boy, who was holding his red arm, and disappeared.

About an hour later I returned to the fish market to leave the wallet somewhere. Sometimes I'll do that so the owner will get back his I.D. and pictures and stuff. It's risky, but I was kind of worried that the kid would get more flack once the father found out his wallet was missing. That peckerhead would get back his credit cards, but not his three hundred dollars in cash. He didn't deserve it.

Then I saw the kid. He was alone, leaning against the wall of a liquor store with his head down. He wasn't crying or anything; in fact he barely moved. Every so often he would stick out the tip of his shoe and grind the concrete, as if he were putting an insect out of its misery. You'd think a little rich kid like that would be all in a panic; instead he was just hanging out as if he didn't belong anywhere or to anyone. I don't know what compelled me, but my feet just sort of walked over to him before I told them to. I put my hands in my pockets and stood next to him.

"Hey, kid, you lost?" The boy looked at me from the corner of his eye but didn't answer. "If you're lost, maybe I can help you." I was acting really crazy, because before I realized what I was saying I asked, "Do you want to come with me?" I heard myself talking and I swear I sounded like a stinking kidnapper. I've never had a problem stealing wallets, but stealing lost kids is out of my territory. It's just that, it must be nice, you know, to be found. Anyway, I figured if he cried or screamed or something, I'd just walk away. He didn't. The kid just nodded his head and peeled himself off the wall.

The kid followed me all the way to my home. I managed to sneak him in the house without Mrs. Alexi seeing me. It didn't really matter since she barely spoke or understood any English and didn't care what I did as long as I paid the rent on time. She was an old lady from Russia with stringy gray hair who spent most of her time making quilts and watching television. For the most part she's a decent lady, but if she saw me on the street I don't think she'd recognize me.

"Make yourself at home, kid." He sat down on my bed looking very uncomfortable. Then the kid did the strangest thing. He took off his cap and with his small hands he folded it in half and smoothed it down, then neatly laid it on the bed next to him. I wasn't sure what to do next.

"Hey, you hungry?" I asked. The kid nodded his head. I went to the kitchen and made a couple of bologna sandwiches and poured a glass of milk. Mrs. Alexi was cool about sharing her food as long as I cleaned up after myself. Even if I ate the whole damn kitchen, as long as I didn't leave any crumbs behind it'd be fine with Mrs. Alexi. I brought the food into my room and watched as the kid nibbled on his sandwich. "So can you talk?"

"Yes," he answered, concentrating on his sandwich.

"Didn't anyone ever tell you never go home with strangers?"

"Yes."

"Then why'd you come home with me?" He just shrugged his shoulders and gulped down his milk. I really didn't know what I was gonna do with him but it was nice having company. Then I had an idea. "D'you wanna see something?"

"Okay." He looked interested, so I wasn't embarrassed when I pulled out a box full of little white pieces of paper. "See, I save these every time I get a fortune cookie. Do you save things?"

"I have some baseball cards."

"Yeah, but these are better. Do baseball cards tell you, 'Love and happiness will be yours in abundance'?"

"No." He giggled. Then he picked one up and read slowly, "'Time is of the es-es-essence, use it wi-se-lee.'"

"Hey, that's a good one," I laughed. "You can keep that."

He loved the fortunes. We spent half the night cracking up over them. The kid was great. He didn't get bored with the fortunes like most kids would. Like me, he seemed to enjoy reading them out loud, and was even eager to see what the next one said, and the next one, and the next one. About eleven o'clock he started getting sleepy, and I found myself getting a little drowsy too. It was a nice, peaceful numbness that I was feeling. I looked at him with his clean hair and clothes and his lopsided smile and I wanted to cry. I never cried, not even when my old man left. All of a sudden, I began gathering the fortunes and stuffing them in a crumpled brown bag.

"I want you to have these, kid. All of these." I was frantic to make sure I got every last one. I opened shoe boxes and dumped hundreds of little pieces of paper into the bag. Then I rummaged through all the back pockets of my pants and pulled out every fortune I could find. I got down on my hands and knees and pulled trash from beneath my bed and sifted through magazines and books and other junk until I got every last slip of smooth paper. "I mean it, kid. I want you to have my fortunes. You know why? You deserve it, kid, you earned it." I pulled one out of the bag. "See this? This old guy named Confuses could predict the future or something. Here it says, 'Long life will be yours.' I want you to have that one especially, because you deserve a long life."

The boy was sitting curled up on the bed looking scared because of my craziness. I didn't mean to scare him, I just wanted him to know what he was worth. I opened my top drawer and grabbed a handful of fortunes and then put them in his lap. "Hey, kid, don't be scared. These are *fortunes.*" The boy hid his face behind a pillow. "I know you think you don't deserve these, but you do. I know what you are, kid. You're tremendous." The next thing I knew tears began to fall down my face. "Do you hear me! Do you? You're special. You're not stupid!" I don't know what came over me but I grabbed his shoulders and shook him. I just wanted to make sure he knew what I was talking about. Really knew. Then the kid was crying too. I pulled him to me and hugged him while I was sobbing like a stinking baby.

"You're tremendous, kid. You have to believe that." I don't know if he understood me because I was crying so hard. Just crying and rocking back and forth saying, "You're tremendous, tremendous."

The next thing I knew it was morning. The kid had rolled over and his arm fell across my face waking me up. I got up and stretched a little. I felt different. I felt good. Today was Monday, the start of a new week. The kid got up next and rubbed his eyes with a clenched fist. He must have forgotten all about last night because he looked at me sleepily and smiled his lopsided smile. I patted his head and smiled too.

"Come on, kid. You ready to go home?" I don't think he was expecting to leave or something because he just looked a little sad. "Don't worry about a thing. You remember what I told you and you'll be okay." I swung him off the bed and put his cap on. I opened the door to leave but the kid was standing in the middle of the room staring at me. "What is it?" I asked.

The kid pointed at the bag full of fortunes. "Can I still have those?"

The tears threatened to come again so I cleared my throat. "Sure.

Sure you can. Didn't I tell you they're yours?" The kid nodded his head and picked up the bag, even stopping to gather the ones that were still scattered on the floor.

I remembered his father's wallet and pulled the driver's license out to see the address. I wasn't surprised to see that he lived in the good part of town. It probably wasn't a smart idea to take him home myself, but I wanted to make sure he got there all right. I took alleys and stayed low until I was a block away from his house.

"That your home? The brick one with the leaves all over the wall?"

"Yeah." He glanced at it uneasily.

"Hey, you're gonna be all right. Just fine. You're tremendous, remember?" The kid nodded and clutched the bag close to him. A lump formed in my throat so I turned quickly down the alley. "Go home now, kid." But he didn't. When I looked over my shoulder I saw him standing in the same position, staring at me with an odd expression on his face. With a final wave, I turned the corner.

The wallet was still in my pocket. I pulled it out and tossed it in a garbage can instead of dropping it somewhere so it could be found and returned. That guy didn't need his credit cards or cash or eelskin wallet. He didn't know what a fortune he had anyway.

FORBIDDEN FATE

Sujata DeChoudhury

The air bit at my skin, inching its way through the tangle of the saffron sari wrapping my body. I tugged at the clinging garment with the sole of my dusty *Bata* sandals but to no avail; the cloth fervently held its grip. The deserted dirt path I walked along in Amalya, a tiny village north of Calcutta, reeked of urine and cow feces. Shops and offices lining the street welcomed my ambling visage with steel, caged faces and signs that screamed in neon letters: XMAS SWEETS and HAPPY XMAS. Brilliant multicolored lights glittered in the doorways beckoning travelers and tourists to savor the sweet sensation of *roshogollas*—curdled balls of sugar and milk—or the spiciest *samosas*—tangy triangles filled with peas and potatoes. A passengerless rickshaw tottered past, the rickshaw *valla* emaciated yet muscular as a result of the heavy loads he'd been hauling since his fifteenth birthday. I knelt down and examined the blister on my left big toe as he passed and then hurried toward the Banerjee *bahrow bahri*—the enormous house of my ancestors.

The deteriorating mansion came into view as I crept around a haggard cow standing in its own dung. Visitors to the house marveled at the immense space of the quarters—five hundred rooms made up the grand total. It must have been beautiful two hundred years ago when weddings flooded the center courtyard gardens and *poojas* brought together Durga Ma worshippers from many kilometers away. I closed my eyes and imagined the squeaking of my *chotis* on the polished wooden floors, the intoxicating smell of fresh white paint on the outer wall of the house drifting in through the high windows, scrubbed and thrown open, and the energetic beat of Hindi songs bouncing in and out of every room, while well-wishers of the bride and groom flirted and feasted in the midst of prosperous families.

The thought made me shudder; for in three days I was to be the decorated wife dressed in the traditional bright red sari and weighed down from head to toe with 24-carat-gold ornaments. Head lowered, lips trembling—I was being sacrificed to an ancient stranger who had met me only once. Five days before the date deemed by the astrologer as an auspicious one for the wedding, I met my future husband—Dr. Sitesh Bhattacharya. Thirty years old, he smiled shrewdly as his beady eyes swept over my still developing frame, never once making contact with mine. Thinning black hair and random silver strands were carefully combed back with noxious hair oil. My grandparents could not be happier; they had raised me since the age of five with a fixed look toward the day when I would submit as a *bohw*—the polite, obedient wife. I showed indifference at this meeting, although I was supposed to show shyness and frailty.

"Savitri, come in here and help prepare dinner," my grandmother greeted me in Bengali as I crossed over to her stool, bent down, and brushed my chapped lips against the tender skin of her cheek.

"Where is Dadu?" I asked as I began to mold and knead the dough she had expertly mixed, bits of flour rising from the generous hump.

"He is watching the television," she replied. Perspiration met in tiny spheres and rolled down the wrinkles around her eyes as she leaned over the firing stove and added ginger and cardamom to the small chunks of goat meat floating in thick curry sauce.

I grasped the burnt wooden rolling pin and proceeded to roll out about twenty circular portions of dough. The deep frying pan sizzled as I dropped them in one by one and watched the *luchees* grow and fluff with air and grease bubbles. A drop of oil jumped innocently from the pan and landed hotly on my neck. I let out a small cry, but quickly stifled it when Dida turned around.

"It is almost done—go fetch your grandfather." She peered at me, her wizened, judging eyes filled with irritation, thinking that a girl of seventeen, let alone a bride in three short days, should be able to cook a simple meal without injuring herself.

Ashamed, I slid out of the fiery chamber and traversed the long, dark corridor, passing empty ghostlike rooms congested with inches of dust and relatives of rats. I detected the mutating glimmer in a square box as I meekly approached the living room. The scrawny servant boy, Arun, who appeared to be some years younger than me—about fifteen—scurried by swiftly carrying a half-empty jug of filtered water. His thin arm brushed mine on his way out the narrow door and drops of water from the clay jug spotted the cloth of my sari. He mumbled an inaudible apology, and my initial disapproving face softened as he lifted his gentle brown eyes framed by never-ending black lashes. I watched through the doorframe as his back vanished into the same prehistoric corridor. He sometimes stayed over when the house was busy with chores and errands to run.

"Dadu, it is suppertime," I said, speaking loudly but gently as I edged closer to the body in the creaking chestnut-colored chair.

"Yes, Savitri—help me up from this broken old chair, will you, please?" he said. His wide black-rimmed glasses hid the softness of his eyes but his voice portrayed it perfectly. The skin under his chin hung over the tight collar of a worn plaid shirt.

I reached over, holding his bony hand tightly as he rose, and we walked arm in arm through the grimy hall and into the kitchen. We perched on the pastel plastic chairs along the edges of the mahogany table that was gradually filled with delicious delectables. Taking Dadu's plate, I piled it with *luchees* and *patah,* the curry sauce of the goat meat seeping into the fried loveliness of the bread. After doing the same for Dida and myself, I settled on the lilac seat and began breaking off bits of my *luchees* and sweeping up *patah,* letting the spices tingle in my mouth until, fully satisfied, I had swallowed the entire scrumptious dish. Arun sat inconspicuously on a straw mat in the corner of the sweltering room, gobbling up the food on his plate as if he would never have the chance to eat again.

Through the cracked glass of the window, we heard the playful cries of neighborhood boys whacking a ball of thread with a wooden stick—their revamped version of cricket. The boy at bat dreamed of being the next Sachin Tendulkar, a living legend and master batsman on the Indian cricket team. While at bat, the lanky boy forgot about his hunger, put aside the chill of a December night without the comfort of a warm blanket, and the shrieks of his mother urging him to do something useful like beg outside the nearby Ram Krishna mission.

I stared out at the boys and reveled in their freedom, in their looseness and impishness. I felt confined in the cloth that pulled around my waist, and trapped in a towering house that radiated images of eroded memories. I closed my weary eyes and breathed in the floating scents of sandalwood, incense, and tired grandparents.

When I was born, my mother cried with tears of glee at the granting of her secret wish to bear a female baby. The first words out of the sneering mouth of Uncle Giri, my mother's brother, were, "Oh, how dreadfully disappointing to have a girl as the firstborn. Now you have to think about dowries, finding a suitable man who will have her, and paying an exorbitant amount of money for her wedding."

My beautiful mother, with round black eyes and long, straight black hair flowing to her lower back, instantly replied, "Well, she doesn't have to get married now, does she?"

"She is pretty like her mother," said my understanding father, nuzzling against his miraculous offspring. They named me Savitri on that blissful day—after a strong woman who had followed her heart in popular Indian folklore.

I vaguely recalled the first six years of my life—most of the memories evoked by torn black-and-white pictures taken by relatives and my parents. I was their only child, which drew much cynicism from the village elders and youth alike. Who would take care of the house after they passed away? Obviously a girl child had no right to property or money. Baba and Ma blatantly ignored pleas to bear another child for the sole purpose of producing a male.

I was lavished with gifts: Cadbury chocolates greeted me on Sunday mornings when I awoke; on the way to my all-girl Montessori school in Rughanam we often stopped by the Kwality ice cream store; little monkeys playing percussion instruments and white-skinned, yellow-haired dolls lined my stuffed shelves. Baba worked for the Congress Party—he usually left at eight in the morning and did not come home until after nine at night. Ma stayed at home and reveled in the gift of a daughter. Her favorite activity involved dressing me up like a little Indian Lady, mixing henna paste and adorning my chubby hands and feet with elaborate patterns of leaves and curves, stirring white paste and decorating my forehead with numerous dots, attacking me with her gold and diamond jewels—shining nose ring, diamond necklaces, colorful bangles, dangly earrings—and cloaking me in gold-trimmed beaded miniature saris. After concocting the perfect Indian Lady, she posed me on the bed and snapped picture after picture, dress after dress, roll after roll.

One Saturday morning, Baba took a surprising day off from work and ushered us to the Calcutta Zoo. As a naïve five-year-old, I cried when the black and brown Bengal tigers roared and the hungry parrots squawked, but giggled when I patted the goat with a beard like my cousin Deepu and laughed when I held the tiny turquoise parakeet that tickled my sweaty palm. Ma had gone to the toilet room and Baba and I were looking for some *foochka* vendors when he released me from his caressing arms and I spotted a fleeting squirrel disappearing into the trees. I teetered after it and found myself surrounded by bushes and greenery. Suddenly alone, I screamed and screamed until Ma rushed through the darkness and swept me into her arms;

Baba followed and promised never to leave me alone again. Never.

One month, two weeks, and three days later, the zoo incident long forgotten, Ma and Baba dressed themselves in their best clothes. Baba had been offered a new job with a growing firm outside Darjeeling and the executives wanted to treat them to dinner in an expensive five-star hotel. They left me home with three of my cousins, two twisted at the ages of fifteen, and the other a simple four-year-old. In a lovely silk fuschia sari and a matching *teep* placed between her eyebrows above the bridge of her long straight nose, Ma glittered like the actresses she showed me from the pages of *Stardust* magazine. A navy blue suit and a maroon tie spotted with white dots completed Baba's debonair appearance. I lost them that night in a freak car accident where a bungling lorry driver crashed and transformed their dwarfish Maruti jeep into an even tinier automobile. I didn't understand that I would never see them again. Ma's parents reluctantly took in the only child—a helpless, pathetic girl—and raised me in the *bahrow bahri* from that day forward.

I opened my eyes and found Dadu and Dida staring into my face, concerned, so I did not bother them with my thoughts. Feigning exhaustion, I bid them sweet dreams, headed to my room, and began to disrobe into my dressing gown. I lay on my bed after climbing into the *moshari* that protected me from bloodthirsty, malaria-stricken mosquitoes who ruled the night. Sweat poured from my skin and the heat overtook my senses even though the creaking fan blew cool air around the tiny room and through the net. In an intoxicated daze, my brain simmering from the warmth, I slipped out of the net and tiptoed from the sweltering cubbyhole.

Candles lit the spiraling staircase I could have traveled blindly. A sharp tiny rock stabbed my foot but I descended without wondering about the gash. I had one destination in mind at this solemn hour. My breaths came fast and hard as I shuffled through the dirt toward the bank of the unused bathing pond that resided within the walls of the sprawling mansion, yet remained open to the starry night. The tiny pebbles massaged my callused feet as I approached the murky wetness. The moonlight captured every ripple in the black liquid. I released the tight braids from my long black hair and shook out the unnatural curls that framed my face. My crisp white nightgown, drenched in dampness from the dull humidity, fell to my ankles, and I waded into the shallow coolness that engulfed me with a welcoming chill. On my back, I floated and stared at the moonlit sky, so vast, so free. I dove under and stayed until my lungs filled beyond their capacity; after finally racing to the surface, I coughed and spattered until the water had drained from my body.

Before the fatal accident, Ma had declared that I was old enough to hear the legend of why relations had stopped swimming in this pond. Hundreds of years ago, my great-great-grandfather's aunt, Karia, had taken her last swim here. It was the wedding day of the eldest daughter in the Banerjee House, Aloka, Karia's sister. At fourteen, Aloka's large black eyes portrayed the confusion of an innocent girl who didn't understand why she had to leave the only home she had ever known, to live with a stranger and his family. She had provided no input; the astrologer and her parents arranged all the wedding plans and festivities. The older girl stayed silent throughout the entire ordeal while a twelve-year-old Karia spent every day until the wedding in Aloka's room. The night before she was to sell her soul to the Chakraborti clan, Aloka quietly packed all her belongings—a worn stuffed elephant, a torn ratty picture of the Goddess Lakshmi, and her cherished red hair ribbons—and stole from the disapproving mansion without a trace and only a few rupees.

The Chakrabortis were furious—no shame like this had ever come to their proud established family. As Brahmins, they were members of the highest caste in India, and had been willing to marry into a lower caste because of the dazzling and much-talked-about beauty of Aloka Banerjee. The Banerjees were horrified by their predicament—they would be considered outcasts in Amalya if the Brahmins placed a curse on their family—and offered the thoughtful Karia in place of the missing bride. At this point, Rahol, the rejected groom, wished for nothing more than a luscious body in his wedding bed that night. With the consent of both families and the marriage astrologer, this new match seemed perfect. No one bothered to ask little Karia what she wanted.

In their twelve years together, Karia developed Aloka's passion for books and they had spent many days under the hot summer sun reading stories from the *Mahabharata* and *Ramayana*. Her beloved sister had left and now Karia was to marry the man Aloka had cast aside. Karia felt trapped; she had wanted nothing more than to one day go to the school down the street and learn more about everything outside these walls. Her mind was filled with heartache for the loss of her sister, and she could not turn to her parents or her brother—they only thought of their good name in the community. She decided to pray to Gayatri Mata—a goddess who enflames the intellectual spirit—and found her body no longer communicated with her soul. In a dazed trance, her feet shuffled briskly toward the murky bathing pond in the center of the rambling palace. Oblivious to the chill of the water, her lithe prepubescent frame vanished into the dark abyss without a struggle. Gayatri Mata welcomed Karia into her magical kingdom with four open arms.

I glanced up and discerned a gray shadow standing very still behind the bars of the balcony. Who could be up at such a late hour? Was it the ghost of Karia? Only *pagol* lunatics and their wives stayed up past midnight, Dadu had told me. The face leaned over—in the darkness I saw the stark profile of a male. I started to ascend from the water, but hastened under the mask of black liquid when I felt the cold air on my naked shoulders. The figure seemed to awake from a dream and vanished just as quickly as he had arrived. I climbed out of the now-freezing water and lifted my nightgown over my head. Fatigue had finally consumed my body as I trudged up the stairs and into my room. I crawled through the mosquito net and collapsed into a comatose sleep.

The next morning, I awoke to find Dida, Dadu, and my Uncle Mithun—the reputable village physician—hovering around the foot of my bed. They had pulled down the protecting net and my uncle was staring intently at a thermometer that I guessed had been resting in my mouth a few moments ago. I peered out the mold-covered window and bright rays of sunlight streaked in—it must have been early after-noon. Arun strode through the door and placed a mug of purified water on my nightstand. His left hand carried a fan; he pulled up a pastel pink chair and began to disturb the heavy air. My grandparents had been concerned about my health since the night before when my thoughts had drifted during the meal and I had gone to bed so early. They grew even more worried when I had failed to wake up. After checking on me and concluding I had a terrible fever, they had called Uncle. The mus-tached man deduced that I was simply overexcited, an emotional sign of the upcoming wedding, and prescribed a day of bedrest and plenty of *jawl*—the water would drain my fever away.

The three adults left and I burrowed my aching head into the cush-ioned comfort of the pillow until I realized that the *chakor* servant was still in the room.

Without lifting my head to look at him I said clearly, "Who gave you permission to watch me bathe?"

"No one, *mehm saab,* Savitri ma'am," he said. I could feel his eyes freeze on me.

"Were you on the balcony last night, *chakor?*" I asked. My anger blossomed into rage as my face turned a brilliant crimson shade.

"Yes, *mehm saab,*" he answered in a calm, even voice.

"You should be ashamed of yourself. So what did you do . . . go brag to all your insignificant friends that you saw a naked girl splash-ing around in a haunted pond in the middle of the night?" This time I turned and held his penetrating gaze.

"No, of course not, Savitri *mehm saab*," he said. He did not even flinch and continued to bring the fan up and down, up and down.

For the first time, I examined this strange young boy who circu-lated in and out of our doorways and had strolled on our floors for the past three months. *Chakors* came and went—at some point they real-ized the opportunities outside the small village and moved up in the world by driving lorries and buses. Wearing a gray short-sleeve button-up shirt and brown half-pants, Arun's tall, lean figure swam in bor-rowed garb. His worn shoes sported miniscule holes behind which I discovered nervous, wriggling toes. I had uncovered the root of his anxiety and where his conscience lay. I scrutinized his innocent, youth-ful face with a button nose and pouty lips; his eyes were dark brown and glittered with speckles of bright green that transfixed me. I lowered my gaze and fell fast asleep to the rhythmic beating of the current pro-duced by the handheld fan.

When I awoke again, I was alone in the room and dusk created an eerie aura over the huts on the steamy horizon. I called for Dida and Dadu but no one answered. Then I remembered that Saraswati Pooja fell on this particular day and they had probably journeyed to the Upanayam Temple. The monstrous house sat in suppressed silence as my hardened feet touched the iciness of the cement. I clutched the lighted candle on my nightstand and traversed the ancient wings of the mansion, dodging cobwebs and sneezing in the primitive dust. Rooms held frames filled with faded black-and-white photographs of family and friends, both equal—merging and meshing into each other. Finally, I stumbled upon the childhood haven of my mother. I pushed open the heavy rotting mahogany door and entered into my own tem-ple. A double bed with intricately carved oak posts rose from the far right corner of the room. An equally exquisite dresser peered at the young intruder through the eye of a tall mirror. Brilliantly blue, dashingly red, and vibrantly orange Rajasthani tapestries covered the stone walls, contributing spurts of energy to the desolate asylum. My grandparents never knew of my visits to this refuge. I stood in front of the one picture that adorned this room—three bodies frozen in a web of endearment at the height of life. Baba clutched a glass of punch in one hand and me, a naked toddler, in the other, his eyes brimming with excitement as confetti dotted his head. Ma grabbed his waist and rested her soft hand on my chubby cheek, her smile overflowing with the joy of a new year.

"Ma," I whispered with tears hanging at the corners of my eyes, "Ma, I want to go away from here. I cannot marry that strange man. I feel like there is something else Shree Krishna wants for me and my feeling is hard to ignore." Her laughing eyes were arrested, nothing stirred in the flickering flame.

The creaking of the door caused me to panic, and I immediately searched for some place to conceal my body from a thief. My breath extinguished the candle and the smoke drifted up and around the many fabrics on the walls.

"*Mehm saab,* you are here? Dadu and Dida wished me to look after you while they worship tonight." Arun's voice filled the chamber with a powerful current of life. Silently, I moved toward the back of his silhouette and touched the soft curve of his neck below the shaggy V of his hair. He froze as I caressed his childish face with the button nose and explored the velvet skin of his cheeks. I found the tiny ridges of his lips and slowly brought my own to his. His untouchable self trembled, such a young creature, plunged into the epiphany of my chaotic dreams. I guided him to the canopied bed of my parents; his voice, lodged in the back of his throat, escaped in sweet, hurried breaths, while my mute voice was elsewhere—speaking, sometimes admonishing, mostly encouraging, from all corners of the room. His inexperienced kisses burned my mouth and began to roam as I shifted my position and allowed his lips to explore. I found his hand and navigated it under the crinkled cotton of my nightgown, brushing against the mounds of unseen breasts and stroking the soft curve of my stomach. My fingers pressed against the small of his back as I breathed in the fresh scent of sandalwood and incense on his skin and in his hair. I burrowed under his body, and for the first time in my life I felt free. I awoke the next morning to find myself in my own room, under the cage of my own mosquito net, fan whirring in the fog of the window—alone.

That night I watched the battered old clock and waited for him to come. Arun did not keep his promise and failed to arrive in my room at our confirmed time. I crept to the right side of Dadu, black-and-white images flashing in front of his hypnotized gaze.

"Where is Arun—I am feeling hot and need some extra breeze," I said. In trying not to show my desperation, I appeared spiteful.

"Did Dida not tell you, Savitri? He took his last rupee and I believe he said he was going to drive a lorry in Bangalore," said Dadu, and never did his compassionate eyes leave the mind-numbing screen. A statue could not have stood more still than I did at that moment. My heart stopped and my breath caught in my dry throat as I shivered at the memory of his gentle, probing touch the night before. I thanked the square box that kept Dadu from seeing the look of despair on my face.

I knew by the sound of his voice that Dadu had not sent him away; nor did Dida. Arun had left on his own whim. Dragging my listless body back to the bed, my mind traipsed in and out of reality and fantasy. Tunneling deeper into the comfort of the stiff mattress, I unearthed a piece of dull yellow scrap paper under my pillow. A note from Arun. He could not defy his India—he had been wrong to step out of place and take advantage of me while I was wallowing in my own sorrow. He had left because he wanted to save me and prayed that the Lord Krishna would forgive me. His written words seemed experienced and toughened—I had stolen his innocence. With the caste system ingrained in his mind, he believed he had sinned against Shiva, and that all destiny would crash if we were together. I had felt it too, but my desire for a life outside these gray cement walls had won the battle against my culture and against my entire family. I could run away, as my ancestor Aloka had done so many years ago, but today there was no way to survive in Calcutta without any money or support. If I ran away, I could become a *chakor* or a whore and scour the streets for morsels of food. I shut my eyes and imagined departing through those heavy front doors, holding the strong, noble hand of Arun and embarking on a splendid life of sweet independence from all-consuming tradition.

Now, running off was a mere passing thought and not one to be acted upon. I would never find him in a country of one billion beings. The gods could be generous, but I knew I had betrayed them at last and could not pray for an answer this time. Under no immediate circumstances could I stay in Amalya and marry a man who looked older than my grandfather and slyer than the Communist Party. I wanted Ma to hold me and tell me that I would always have her. I prayed that she would come back, and my body shook in sobs as I realized that the gods were probably ignoring all of my pleas. My legs started to move; my physical motions no longer connected to the weighty emotions saturating my thoughts. Bearing half a heart, my mind swam with distant, lovely sentiments as I followed in the fatal footsteps of Queen Karia.

Luminescent, brilliant hues of the aurora embraced her entrance. The air, the light, the atmosphere surpassed all of her earlier feelings. She looked calmly over the clouds and murmured into the tiny ears of the passing seagulls. The waves of the clear ocean crashed against the rainbows of the thick coral reef, painting the sunrise that crept up on the grand horizon. Her blue-black hair sparkled in the soaring sun that finally found a peaceful home behind the colossal mountain. A simple white piece of cloth covered her lilting figure, tied with a pearly sash that flowed past her knobby knees. She laughed aloud when a baby seagull stopped to rest upon her naked shoulder. Her breaths came short and sweet; her chest rose and fell to the gentle laps of water lagging behind on the sand after the great wave disappeared. Rising and falling, ascending and descending—the swirling air rushed around her body and swept her up in an eternal embrace, while Gayatri Mata smiled upon a creation who had reached nirvana at last.

William Clifford has traveled and held many different jobs since graduating from Carnegie Mellon University. To (barely) pay the bills, he holds cue cards at *Late Show with David Letterman* and *Saturday Night Live* in New York City, which he calls home. He is a staff writer at www.thicksole.com, and is at work on a novel.

Matthew Loren Cohen grew up in South Florida and graduated from Florida State University with a BA in music. "Polaroid" was written in 1997 as the third part in a trilogy of short stories. His work has appeared in Blithe House Quarterly, a Web site for gay short fiction (www.blithe.com). He lives in New York City.

Sujata DeChoudhury, a native of Greensburg, Pennsylvania, is a Systems and Control Engineering major at Case Western Reserve University in Cleveland, Ohio. "Forbidden Fate" is dedicated to her loving *Dida* and *Dadu,* who breathe Calcutta every day of their lives.

Dennis G. Dillingham, Jr., was born and raised in Long Island and is the youngest of five children. He is a graduate of the College of the Holy Cross, where, in 1998, he received a BA degree with honors. He has also studied literature and history at the University College Galway, in Galway, Ireland. He currently lives in Hoboken, New Jersey, and works in New York City.

Alsha D. Gayle attends Yale University. She has been featured in publications at Columbia University, Yale University, and most recently in *Chocolate for a Young Woman's Soul* (Fireside/Simon & Schuster). She teaches creative writing in a New Haven elementary school, is Marketing Director of Yale's undergraduate style magazine, *vyrtigo,* writes for the *Yale Daily News,* and is the sweeper on her women's club soccer team.

Clementyne Howard attends college in Nashville, Tennessee. Her father, Harlan Howard, is a brilliant songwriter whose passion and gift for words inspires her to search within for the same. She is currently studying television and writing.

Kathleen Bedwell Hughes was born and raised in Indianapolis, Indiana. She received her BA in English from Yale University in 1994 and her MFA from the University of Iowa Writer's Workshop in 1998. She is currently at work on a novel..

Carmen Elena Mitchell grew up in Chicago and attended Sarah Lawrence College in New York. Now based in Seattle, she makes a living writing, acting, and teaching. Her work has appeared in *The Sow's Ear, The Seattle Medium,* and has been heard nationally on KidStar radio. She is currently at work on a novel.

Jason Rekulak grew up in New Jersey. He has an MFA from the University of Miami, where he received a full scholarship from James Michener. He currently lives in Philadelphia with his wife, Julie, and is finishing a collection of short stories about newspaper personal ads.

Michelle Rick has a BA in literature and creative writing from Northwestern University and is currently a candidate for an MFA in Creative Writing from the New School University. Her fiction has been published in the *Mississippi Review, Moondance Magazine, Exquisite Corpse,* and an anthology, *Summer's Love, Winter's Discontent.* She is working on a collection of short stories and a novel and lives in Greenwich Village.

Davy Rothbart received nine Hopwood Awards, the Arthur Miller Prize, and a Lawrence Kasdan Fellowship at the University of Michigan. Current writing projects include a road novel and a biography of Vietnam Veteran James A. Thompson. With his film company, 21 Balloons Productions, he has completed two documentaries, *Coast II Coast* and *Where Is the Friend's Home?* Also, he once tossed up an -oop to Jalen Rose in a pickup game. His story is dedicated to the writers at Cotton Correctional Facility, Jackson, Michigan.

Joy Monica T. Sakaguchi, a Los Angeles native, currently lives in Alaska, where she works with senior citizens. In her free time she enjoys exploring Alaska, keeping warm, hiking, writing, and painting.

Chandra Steele is from Great Neck, New York, and attended Barnard College, where she was editor-in-chief of the *Barnard Bulletin.* She is currently a copy editor and is working on a short story collection and a screenplay.

Aury Wallington lives in Manhattan. She works as a script coordinator on the HBO show *Sex and the City,* and spends all of her free time working toward her black belt in karate.

Martin Wilson was born in Tuscaloosa, Alabama, and educated at Vanderbilt University and the University of Florida. In 1999, a story of his appeared in *Virgin Fiction 2* (Rob Weisbach Books/Morrow). He lives and works in Austin, Texas.

As many as one in three
Americans with HIV...
DO NOT KNOW IT.

More than half of those
who will get HIV this year...
ARE UNDER 25.

HIV is preventable.
You can help fight AIDS.
Get informed. Get the facts.

www.knowhivaids.org
1-866-344-KNOW

Like this is the only one...

Floating
Robin Troy

Door to Door
Tobi Tobin

The Fuck-up
Arthur Nersesian

A Hip-Hop Story
Heru Ptah

Dreamworld
Jane Goldman

Fake Liar Cheat
Tod Goldberg

Dogrun
Arthur Nersesian

Brave New Girl
Louisa Luna

The Foreigner
Meg Castaldo

Tunnel Vision
Keith Lowe

Number Six Fumbles
Rachel Solar-Tuttle

Crooked
Louisa Luna

Don't Sleep with Your Drummer
Jen Sincero

Thin Skin
Emma Forrest

Last Wave
Paul Hayden

More from the young, the hip,
and the up-and-coming.
Brought to you by MTV Books.

© 2004 MTVN

POCKET
BOOKS

The Alphabetical Hookup List

A–J
K–Q
R–Z

Three sizzling titles
Available from
PHOEBE McPHEE
and MTV Books

www.mtv.com

www.alloy.com

Praise for Stephen Chbosky's
THE PERKS OF BEING A WALLFLOWER

"A coming-of-age tale in the tradition of *The Catcher in the Rye* and *A Separate Peace*. . . . [Chbosky's] poignant reflections on life, love, and friendship are often inspirational and always beautifully written."

—*USA Today*

"Charlie's loving instincts are very strong. Again and again throughout the book he exhibits that pure wisdom we all like to read about and witness. And Stephen Chbosky doesn't let us down. The language is plain and springy and blunt. . . . In this culture where adolescence is a dirty word, I hope nothing bad ever happens to this [protagonist]."

—*Los Angeles Times*

"An epistolary narrative cleverly places readers in the role of recipients of Charlie's unfolding story of his freshman year in high school. From the beginning, Charlie's identity as an outsider is credibly established. . . . Charlie, his friends, and his family are palpably real . . . [he] develops from an observant wallflower into his own man of action. . . . This report on his life will engage teen readers for years to come."

—*School Library Journal* (starred review)

"Chbosky captures adolescent angst, confusion, and joy as Charlie reveals his innermost thoughts while trying to discover who he is and who he is to become. Intellectually precocious, Charlie['s] . . . reflections . . . are compelling. He vacillates between full involvement in the crazy course of his life and backing off completely. Charlie is a likable kid whose humor-laced trials and tribulations will please both adults and teens."

—*Booklist*

"Chbosky adds an upbeat ending to a tale of teenage angst—the right combination of realism and uplift to allow it on high school reading lists. . . . [The protagonist] oozes sincerity, rails against celebrity phoniness, and feels an extraliterary bond with his favorite writers (Harper Lee, Fitzgerald, Kerouac, Ayn Rand, etc.). . . . A plain-written narrative suggesting passivity, and thinking too much, lead to confusion and anxiety."

—*Kirkus Reviews*

An Amazon.com #1 Young Adult Bestseller
Available from MTV Books/Pocket Books